Last Chance TOWN

Further Adventures Along the Road Without End

Hey John;
Please enjoy the ride,
and thanks!
Big hugs,
Ron Kearse

Ron Kearse

Last Chance Town

Front Cover Photograph Courtesy of:
City of Vancouver Archives
City of Vancouver–AM 1 502 S1-2-: CVA 1502-307
Vandusen Botanical Garden Association
Vancouver, British Columbia
Canada

Tellwell Talent
www.tellwell.ca

ISBN
978-0-2288-3143-3 (Hardcover)
978-0-2288-3145-7 (Paperback)
978-0-2288-3144-0 (eBook)

To my late partner, Steven Carl Foster, who passed away on July 31, 2015. I was almost through the first draft of this book when you were suddenly gone. I dedicate this book to you. For thirty years, you supported me in everything I did and every whim I had. I'll always remember the many fun places in the world we visited and all the fun times we shared. Love Always, Ron.

Acknowledgement

It is with deep respect that I acknowledge the incarcerated Indigenous men and women throughout Canada and the employees and volunteers who work within the Canadian Corrections System. I worked with Indigenous offenders and their Corrections Teams for eight years; and none of them will know the lessons they taught me about life and most of all, being human.

Through my experiences working with incarcerated Indigenous men and women, I have truly come to learn that criminals are not born, they're made… and they're human!

I listened to the offenders' life stories and the events in their lives that led them to incarceration. I worked with them, their Elders, and their families, and I noticed there were common threads in each of the stories of their lives. They recounted stories of physical and sexual abuse from the time they were children. Neglect, drug addiction, alcoholism, street life, the constant threat of violence that all led them to the same end… prison. Much of this abuse stemming from the effects, direct and residual, of the Residential School System.

Let me be clear, I am not excusing the actual crimes these offenders committed. Most of them fully understand they inflicted a lot of hurt on people, sometimes with brutal and interminable results. And even though I do agree there are some offenders who *should* stay imprisoned indefinitely, I have come to know that most deserve a shot at redemption. That's all many of them are asking for, a chance to make things right, somehow.

This is Warren Givens's story. His character is inspired by all those common threads from the lives of the incarcerated Indigenous men and women I've worked with. I hope that I have given them the respect due them for all their efforts working for the day their shot at redemption becomes real life.

Niá:wen kowa;

Ron Kearse

Haudenosaunee (Mohawk) Ancestry:
Six Nations of The Grand Territory

Last Chance TOWN

Further Adventures Along the Road Without End

PART FIVE

May 1988 – Warren Givens

Sometimes these lunch shifts at Enzo's are brutal! The name of this place is Enzo's, and it's been fucking busy from the time I started till now. The restaurant is closed for a couple of hours while the rest of the staff clean up and get ready for the dinner shift. I take a swig of the beer that I got from the bar.

This is my day gig. When I'm not writing for my book, I'm here or at my favourite watering hole, the Castle Pub. I've gotten to know so many people who go there regular-like, that I just know whenever I go there, I'll see somebody I know.

Anyways, Enzo, the owner of this place, always lets us have one drink from the bar when our shifts are over, especially when it's the lunch shift like this, "but you've gotta save some for the customers," he'll say with a grin.

He'll usually let us play the radio between shifts. "Sweet Dreams" by Eurythmics is playing, and the memories are flooding back. When this song was popular, me, Gil, and Neil took that holiday from Calgary to Vancouver, and it was fantastic! Man, I'll never forget that trip as long as I live.

I remember I was sleeping in the back seat of the car when Gil woke me up.

"Hey, sleeping beauty, we're here," he said. Then he pointed to the North Shore Mountains.

I remember getting all excited and asking Neil to turn on some music, and this was the song that we heard. I was ready to party! Yep, that trip changed my life… in too many ways.

I also remember the two of them warning me about heading down to Wreck Beach that morning with Ray and Paul, two guys I met at the bar one night. But I didn't listen and did things my way, went down to sell some dope, and ended up in jail to think about it… again! So much for knowing better than everyone else.

I never saw Gil and Neil again. Funny how one dumb-ass decision can change your life for good! These days though, I keep a secret stash of the shit just to keep my ass above water. Some say I'll never learn, but I don't give a shit. I have a few trusted, happy customers and the extra, tax-free cash is nice to have. I'm silent as I wonder what Gil's up to now. I heard he tried to see me when I was at the remand downtown, but a couple of the screws gave him a major hassle, so he just dropped my shit off and left. I'm guessing he went back to Toronto with Neil. They always did like each other.

I got out of jail in 1986, and I've been keeping my head down as much as I can this time. I've had it with jail—Clown College! The guys inside go on and on about being solid, being loyal, being someone worth trusting. But that don't mean shit! They'd all sell you down the river given half the chance… except Gil. Christ, I still miss him. Now *there* was one solid guy! I tried to get hold of him when I was first let out, but I didn't even know where to begin! So that was that. I only hope the best for you, buddy, wherever you ended up. I want you to fuckin' know that I'm missing the hell out of you.

I figured out I liked working in the kitchen, helping out and doing some cooking and shit wile I was inside. Carol, my probation officer, helped me get into a cooking course that the slam was offering when I was finally getting close to ending my sentence. Because I had my GED, I worked part time at a small greasy spoon when I got released.

Then not long after, I answered an ad for a full-time cook and that's when I met Enzo. He's owned and operated this joint for almost twenty years, and I don't know how the old bugger does it, God love him. He'll always be the top guy in my books. When other people saw me as just another ex-con, Enzo took me under his wing. I'm figuring that's because one of his brothers was in jail back in Italy. Enzo saw how other folks in the town treated him when he got out. So, Enzo treats me like a son. He's one bonus guy.

Him and his wife, Sylvana, came over to Canada from Calabria in Italy back in the early sixties, and he built this business from nothing. The two of them go to church every Sunday and give part of their pay to the Catholic Church every month… shit, there's a loud clatter in the kitchen and Enzo's flipping out again. *"You stoopid son-a-ma-bitch! I work hard running a business and you want to give me a heart attack!"*

All this over a couple of broken plates, but that's Enzo.

He has a son Celso, and he's going for an engineering degree at university. On one hand that pleases Enzo, but Celso isn't interested in the business, and Enzo takes it personally. He was hoping Celso would take the business over when he retires.

While I'm finishing off the bottle, Will comes in from the kitchen and joins me at the table. Will is one of the other cooks, and he's a real odd duck. Nice enough guy, but still an odd duck.

I remember once he phoned me at home, right out of the blue! He wanted to know if he and his boyfriend could buy some pot from my stash. We had talked one day, and he said him and his boyfriend liked smoking dope, so I mentioned my stash to him.

So anyways, he phones me up out of the blue wanting to know if him and Bob, his boyfriend could buy some. I said sure, then I could hear Bob yelling in the background that he's leaving to come over to get it right away. Will had me on the phone for so long that Bob showed up at my door, got the pot, and arrived back at their place while Will still told me sad stories about his life. They live in New Westminster, one of Vancouver's suburbs, about a three quarters of an hour drive from my place! He yakked on the phone for an hour and a half! I always thought those two are in serious needs of lives.

Anyways, back at the restaurant, Will's starting in with his usual whining about how life's a shit sandwich when Enzo comes into the main area of the restaurant and sees us at the table.

"You two still here? Don't ya have homes ta go to? Go on, get outta here." He motions with his hands. "We'll be openin' for dinner soon."

I laugh, swallow the last of the beer, put the empty bottle in a beer case behind the bar, say my see-ya-laters to everyone, then leave the restaurant. Since tomorrow's my day off, I'll check out what's going on over at the watering hole. Who knows? Maybe I can even get laid or something. I light a cigarette and take a drag as I walk up to Granville Street.

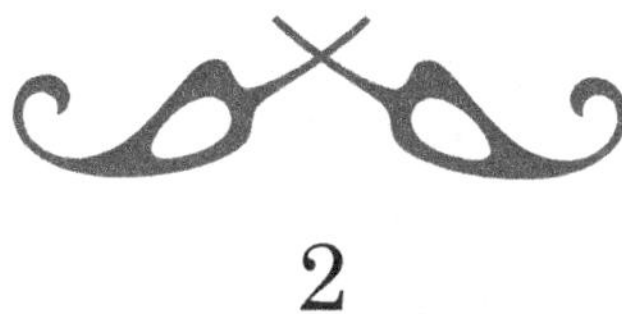

2

There's something fuckin' lonely about sitting in a bar when most of the crowd hasn't arrived yet. It's only seven o'clock on a Friday night and I'm sipping on another beer.

Meantime, just behind me I hear five old queens sitting at the bar bitchin' about this and grousing about that. Those five old fuckers are here every week and all they do is get drunk and moan. *"My next lover is gonna like classical music."* -or- *"My next boyfriend isn't gonna dress like a slob!"* Take some advice bitches, get a dog! It's the only thing that'll be everything you want it to be!

I take another drag of my half-smoked cigarette while Van Halen are belting out "Panama" on the jukebox by the back exit. I love this song! It fuckin' kicks ass!

Meantime, for the last hour or so I've been watching a band of Natives setting up their music equipment on the small stage in the corner of the room. Now they look like they're ready to start playing at any moment. The guy on lead guitar reminds me of one of my uncles. He was a big guy and wore his hair in braids like this guy is. My uncle liked to play guitar too, he was really into country music. Chet Atkins and Roy Clark were his heroes.

Been a while since I even thought about him and them cousins of mine. *White Eyes* they used to call me because I got white skin like my old man. "Go back to the city, White-Eyes," they'd say. Got so I didn't wanna see them anymore, so I didn't.

Just as the music on the jukebox fades to the end of the song, the band on stage starts the opening chords of their first set for the night. A cover of "Walk of Life" by Dire Straits.

Meantime, I notice a guy who's just come into the pub from the alley entrance. He's sitting at a table close to the jukebox and looking around the room as the evening crowd's trickling back into the bar after dinner. I've seen him in here before, but I don't know his name or nothing.

We make eye contact, and the more I look at him, the more he's making me hard.

He's a fuckin' good looking bastard, broad-shouldered, tall with longish, blond hair. He kind of reminds me of Daryl Hall from Hall and Oates, except he's got a bushy, droopy blond moustache and fucking wicked blue eyes. I don't fucking know why I'm still sitting here when a two-hour love affair is sitting by the jukebox waiting to be had.

Terry, the bar's manager stands at my side holding his cigarette in one hand while his other hand's tucked inside his pants pocket. He smiles at me.

"Night off tonight?" he says raisin' his voice, and slightly bent over to me so I can hear him over the music.

"Yeah," I yell back, "did a lunch shift today."

"Where's your roommate, Don?"

"It's his payday so he's probably back at home putting together a new music tape." We're silent for a moment. Then, "Hey Terry, I always wanted to ask you something?"

"What's that?"

"You've been sober for a few years now…"

"Yeah."

"Don't it bother you that you're surrounded by alcohol every day?"

He raises one eyebrow like Mr. Spock would. "Sometimes," he says, "but then every day I watch normally rational guys turn into idiots after a few drinks, and that always reminds me of why I stay sober."

"Ever get tempted to drink again?"

"That never goes away. But like I say, I just watch what happens with a lot of these guys every week, and that gives me good reason to stay sober."

"You must have seen it all here."

He smirks. "If these walls could talk."

The band is now going full tilt into their song.

"These guys are pretty good," I say. "They sound almost like Dire Straits. Where they from?'

"Northern BC, Kitimat, I think."

"You should invite them back soon."

"We'll see. The roster is pretty booked for the next few months."

Then he makes a sweeping motion with his hand over the growing crowd. "See anything you like here?"

"Well, see that hot guy sitting over by the jukebox with the blond hair and moustache?"

"Yeah, his name's Daryl," says Terry. "He's a musician."

"I knew I'd seen him before! He's played here before, hasn't he?"

"You bet."

"'I always thought that he looks like that musician Daryl Hall."

Terry looks at him closely. "Yep, I guess he does look a bit like him."

"Anyways, Mr. Daryl and me have been eyein' each other since he came in."

"You like that, d'ya?"

"Yeah!"

"I'm surprised you're not over there chattin' him up." Terry laughs. "That's not like you to be shy."

Then one of the waiters, comes over. "Hey Terry, can I talk to you for a moment?" Terry nods and they go through a door into his office behind the bar.

That's when Daryl gets up from his table and comes up to the bar. It looks like he's going to order a beer but then he turns to me. "Wanna go out for a toke?"

I've played this game long enough to know that question always leads to sex.

"Hell, yeah," I say. So, I follow him out the back door and into the alley.

"I'm Daryl," he says.

"I'm Givens."

"Good to meet you, Givens," he says as we shake hands.

"Likewise."

We reach a red brick archway overhanging a back door in the alley and duck in. He takes out a joint, has a toke, and passes it to me.

"Here, blow this," he smiles and winks.

"I'd rather be blowin' you," I say, takin' the joint and having a toke.

He chuckles, puts his hand behind my head, and kisses me, deeply… then deeper. He smiles. "Follow me."

I butt out the joint on the wall, as he takes a penknife out of his pocket and sticks it in a small lock in the door. I hear something click, and we walk through the back-service door of the Castle Hotel.

"You picked that lock like a fuckin' expert," I say quietly. He smiles and puts his finger in front of his mouth, *Shhh.* He takes my hand and pulls me up a back staircase, we get to the landing between the third and fourth floors (I think), where we continue kissing and get each other's pants down to our ankles. I'm feeling his thick cock as it grows while I tug on it. He cups my balls and strokes my cock while we kiss. We're really getting into each other when we hear a door open somewhere below us in the stairwell. We immediately pull up our pants and straighten ourselves out.

Then we hear footsteps on the stairs. Another door opens. The footsteps disappear and then the door closes.

Silence.

Daryl looks at me. "Wanna continue this at my place?"

"Fuckin' right."

We go back down the stairs out into the alley. "Let's get a cab," he says.

"Sure."

He goes to a small bank of phones at the back exit of the bar and makes the call.

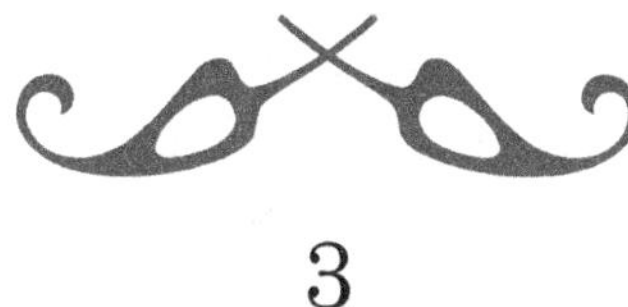

3

We take a cab to where Hastings-Sunrise meets Grandview-Woodlands in East Vancouver. We get out of the cab and go up the front walk to his place. It's an older house, two storeys, blue and grey. Looks like it could use a little TLC as far as repair work goes. We enter the front hall. There's music coming from the kitchen.

"Ah, the roomie's home," he says pointing at the pair of runners in the front closet. "You want something to drink?"

"Sure."

We take off our shoes.

"This way," he says as he leads me into the kitchen. Somewhere Tom Jones is singing "Kiss" as part of the Art of Noise cover.

We pass a large, framed poster on the wall in the hallway. I stop to have look at it. It's square and features a red background with a black bull within a circle of words that read, *Transcend the Bullshit.* Makes me chuckle.

In the kitchen, we're greeted by a guy in his underwear doing what looks like ballet moves. Daryl glances at him. "You're drinking red wine again?"

"When have I stopped?" His roommate answers as he twirls across the kitchen floor.

"Givens, this is Hunter," Daryl says pointing at him.

"Good to meet you." I wave as he twirls out of the kitchen into the dining room, and that's when we hear ka-THUNK!

Daryl sprints into the dining room with me right behind him.

"You okay?" Daryl asks.

Hunter gets up from the floor, laughs then shakes my hand. "Good to meet you too." Then he twirls around and out of the room then bolts upstairs.

"Christ," I say, "I want some of whatever Hunter's been smokin'."

"Yeah," says Daryl with a wry smile, "you've entered another universe. But don't worry about it, you'll fit in just fine."

4

The smoke detector going off just about makes me shit!

"WHAT THE FUCK!" I yell as I spring naked from the bed.

"It's just Hunter in the kitchen," says Daryl. "He forgot about his toast again."

After a few seconds the smoke detector stops screeching and Hunter yells, "Sorry guys!"

"S'alright!" Daryl yells back.

I can hear Rick Astley the radio down in the kitchen singing "She Wants to Dance with Me." And it sounds like Hunter is dancing around the kitchen.

I settle back into bed and look around Daryl's bedroom. I see a Roland keyboard sitting at one end of the room with a guitar resting against one side of it. A small stack of sheet music and a mini-moog synthesizer are sitting on top of it. I look along the walls at bright coloured paintings of different sizes.

"Did you paint them?" I ask pointing at the wall closest to us.

"I used to, it amused me."

"I like 'em. I like the colours. Did you go to art school or somethin'?"

"Thanks. I was going to go to art school and learn graphic design, but I didn't."

"Why?"

"I took music instead."

"I sure like your paintings. So, ya' don't paint no more?"

"Nope."

"You're a musician instead?" I ask.

"Yep."

"I seen ya play at the Castle before. You're good."

"Thanks, I appreciate that. Yeah, sometimes I play piano while a lady friend of mine sings. It's something we've done for a few years, and we don't do it often, but we both enjoy it. Mostly, my friends and I have put together a band and do various gigs around town."

"Answer me somethin'."

"What's that?"

"Last night when we were blowin' tokes in the alley..."

"Yeah."

"Come clean, you *did* pick that lock like an expert."

Daryl smiles. "How would you know that?"

"I've done time in the slam."

He smiles. "Okay, you're right. I did some time for B and E in my youth. What were you in for?"

"Possession for purposes of trafficking and resistin' arrest."

We're both silent for a moment.

"We've got something in common then." Daryl smirks.

"Yeah, I guess we do. So how long did you spend inside?"

"Ten months. That's when I decided I didn't like the path I was on, so went back to high school, got my diploma, then went to San Francisco and university. How about you?"

"I had a small gig going on in Edmonton sellin' pot and ended up inside. When I got out, I came out here on vacation with a couple of buddies and started sellin' the shit again, got caught, back to jail."

"Hmm, didn't quite get it the first time?"

"Guess not," I say. "I still keep a small stash just in case I get stuck for money again."

We're both silent. Daryl shrugs it off.

"I'll know where to go to get my stuff then." He grins.

"Sure thing." I smile. "Anyways, what does Hunter do?"

"He's a dancer," Daryl says.

"No shit."

"Yeah, and a good roommate. By the way, we're looking for another roommate. Know anybody who's looking to move?"

"Maybe," I say. "My roommate told me the other day, that him and his boyfriend wanna move in together soon. But he didn't give me a date, so I'll probably be lookin' soon."

We're silent again while I'm staring at him.

"What?" he asks.

I lay a lip lock on him like there's no next week. I kiss down his chest, cover myself with the blankets and go down on him.

5

It's later in the morning and both of us have had our showers and something to eat. Daryl's put on the radio while we've having another cup of coffee.

"So, you a Vancouver boy?" I ask.

"Nah, I was born in Hawaii."

"Cool! What part?"

"Honolulu. My old man was working at the navy base there."

"Was he in the navy?"

"No, he was a civilian worker. I moved to California in 1971 to go to university. I thought that as long as I stayed in school my name wouldn't come up with the draft board... until it did. I didn't want to leave San Francisco, because I was twenty-two years old, and had just come out of the closet. I was getting into the whole west-coast-gay-lifestyle thing that I didn't want to let go of. And I sure as hell wasn't going to go to war for some tinpot politician like Nixon!"

"So, you packed your shit and moved here to Vancouver?"

"That's pretty much how it happened. I had a couple of friends who made up their minds to come here too, and for the same reasons as me. So, here I am."

"Musta been tough."

"That's what a lot of people back home don't get. Many of them thought I was some kind of coward and it was easy for me to pack up and go. But I didn't believe we had any reason to be in Viet Nam in the first place. So, even though it was an easy decision for me to make, it was really hard to pack and move to another country to start all over again. I thought that I would probably never come back home. If I did, I'd risk going to jail again. I lost friends and the support of family members because of it, especially my parents."

"Really? Your parents don't talk to you no more?"

"Sad but true. But I don't regret my decision at all." He shakes his head slowly. "Not at all."

"So, you still can't go back to the States?"

"Oh, I could now if I want to. The draft ended by the mid-seventies, and then an amnesty for the conscientious objectors was put in place. I miss Hawaii, and I miss my parents and family, but I don't want to go back. I'm happy here."

I notice the music playing on the radio.

"What's this we're listenin' to?"

"CiTR 101.9," he says, "out of UBC."

I'm quiet for a second. "The university has a radio station?"

"Yep. You've never heard of it?"

I shrug, then listen again.

"Who's singin'?

"It's a group from Iceland called the Sugarcubes."

"It's weird. Ain't you a little too old to be listening to shit like this?"

He laughs.

"You're only too old if you believe you're too old. And besides, why listen AM Radio, when there's a whole world of different types of music out there?"

"I like Dire Straits and Springsteen better."

"You're forgiven," he says.

"Yeah, up yours too."

"Since I didn't give you a tour of the place last night, want one now?"

"Sure."

It's a three-bedroom old house in East Vancouver, and it's seen better days.

"The folks who lived here before us were here for twenty-seven years. They pretty much desecrated this place."

"Yeah, I can kinda see that," I say pointing to the cheap wall paneling in the living room.

Daryl smirks and nods his head. "Yeah, this place was built in 1910, and there was wainscoting throughout the main floor. They tore that out, put in that cheap shit paneling and then bricked over some beautiful emerald green tile around the fireplace there. If you look closely through the grout, you can see it. It's pretty sad."

I lean over and look through the pieces of broken grout on the fireplace.

"You're right," I say looking at the tile behind the brick. "So, just the two of you live here?"

"There used to be three of us and unfortunately with our third roommate having moved out, it makes things a little harder for Hunter and me to pay the rent. We don't want to give the place up."

He shows me the empty bedroom on the main floor, and I think, *Hmm, even though Don and his boyfriend ain't made any solid plans yet, the idea of moving to the east end and sharin' a house instead of an apartment seems like a good one to me. Maybe I could use a change.*

"Y'know," I say while looking around the room, "on second thought, *I'm* interested in movin' in with ya. What's the rent here?"

"Six-fifty a month."

"Wow. We're payin' five fifty for a two-bedroom apartment in the West End. What are the bills every month?"

"Your share would be about twenty or thirty a month. Depending on the season."

"That's only a little more than my share of the rent and bills in the West End, and that's just for a fuckin' two-bedroom apartment!"

"Yeah," says Daryl as we walk back into the kitchen, "living here you've got a whole house, plus a back yard with a big deck."

I look around. "This is a real party kitchen."

"We've had a few good ones here."

"Yeah? A few good orgies too, I'll bet."

Daryl grins and arches his eyebrows.

I look out the patio doors to the deck outside. I can see myself out there in the summer on my time off, and the idea of a party kitchen complete with a big outside deck suddenly grabs me.

"Tell you what," Daryl says, "it would help us out a lot if you seriously considered a move here because to be honest, we've been thinking of posting a public notice for a roommate, and we really don't want to do that."

"The thing is," I say, "you don't even know me."

"That's okay. You don't know me either."

"I could be some kinda fuckin' nutcase…"

"And I could be some fuckin' sex psycho."

"I could be your worst nightmare," I say.

"And I could be the best roomie you've ever had." Daryl grins.

Silence for a moment as we smile at each other.

"What about pets?"

"You got one?"

"A cat."

"Hunter had one too when he first moved in, and the landlord didn't know a thing."

"He doesn't have the cat anymore?"

"It got sick and had to be put down."

"Oh." I'm silent for a moment. "Y'know, this is happenin' pretty fast."

"You'll need the time to give your roommate notice," says Daryl.

I laugh out loud. "You're a fuckin' good salesman."

"I'm a musician, I gotta be."

"What's the landlord like?"

"He's a bit of an asshole, but nothin' I can't handle."

"How do you mean *asshole*?"

"He comes on to me every once in a while."

"You mean like, he wants to have sex with you?"

"Yeah, but I tell him he's bein' boring again and he laughs, and that puts a stop to it… until the next time it happens."

"He's gay then?"

"A frustrated old queen. As far as he's concerned, any cock will do."

"Why do you put up with that?"

"Because the rent is good, and he's good with any repairs that have to be done, and besides, if you treat it like a game, things aren't bad at all."

I've got a really good feeling about this. We talk about it for a little while, and before I know it, I agree that I'll be letting my roommate know about this so we can give our month's-notice to the landlord.

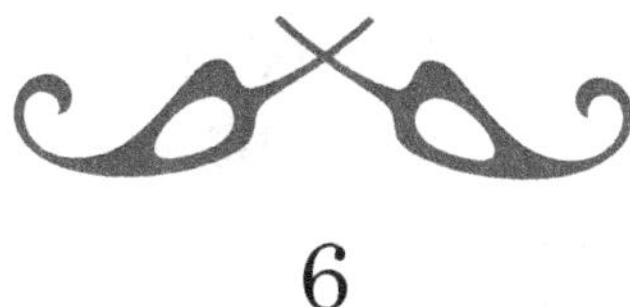

6

I walk through the West End toward the corner of Bidwell and Nelson Streets, when I pass that house, the one that everyone on the block knows.

We all call her *the Porch Lady*. That's because she lives on her fuckin' front porch! I ain't shitting you! Anytime I walk by her place, there she sits watching soap operas, *Matlock*, Dallas, *St. Elsewhere*, or some other shit. Even in the fuckin' winter she sits there bundled up in a big easy chair watching the fuckin' TV on her porch! Her front door is always wide open, so I peek inside when I walk by to see stacks of bundled newspapers and boxes piled almost to the ceiling. No wonder she lives on the porch! There ain't no room for her in the fuckin' house! She never speaks to anyone, I never seen anyone visit her—she just sits on her front porch watching the TV eating something.

I get into the apartment, and just like I told Terry at the bar last night, Don's sitting cross-legged in front of the stereo doing his usual payday thing, recording a tape. We wave to each other, and he takes off his headphones.

"Have you been there all night long?" I ask.

"No. I went to bed about midnight and got up to finish this tape about an hour ago."

He's got this fucking amazing collection of records and tapes, and he's got milk crates full of records in his bedroom. He doesn't drink very much, and the only time he goes out is with his boyfriend Jerry and the few buddies they have. He's pretty quiet… okay, he's boring as shit, but we get along well, and he will have the occasional toke.

That usually makes him loosen up a little. I don't know Jerry, pardon me, *Jerome* very well, and he doesn't come around all that much. But anytime he does, he's one of the most opinionated shits I've ever heard. Talk about thinking his shit don't stink!

He's an A-List Gay. You know the type, dresses well and has a well-paying job, pardon me, *career!* I remember this one time he was over and started shit-talking, as usual. He was going on about how only *little people* have *jobs*, but one must have a *career* to have respect. I can't stand the fucker. He lives in the *la-tee-dah* part of town, Kitsilano. Whatever! I put up with him because of Don.

Ozzy, my big black and white cat, rubs up against my legs wanting attention. He followed me home one day and has been a good buddy to me ever since. I give him a rub behind his ears. He's a six-year-old Maine-coon according to the vet, and he's fucking huge! About the size of a mid-sized dog! I guess he weighs in twenty or twenty-five pounds. The thing I like most about Ozzy is he'll be your buddy, but there's no fucking way he'll be your baby. I hear ya Oz, I hear ya. He purrs.

"Anyway, I'm glad you're home," I say. "I've got something I have to tell ya."

"What is it?"

"You know you told me that you and Jerry we're thinkin' of movin' in together?"

"Yeah."

"I kinda took that and ran with it."

"What do you mean?"

"I found a place to move into the end of next month."

He looks a little stunned. "This is rather sudden! Where you movin' to?"

"I'll be sharin' a house with a guy over on the East Side. Hey, I know this is real sudden notice, and I'm real sorry about that. But this is somethin' that's landed on my lap, and I want to take it."

Don's quiet while he's thinking about what he's hearing. "Okay," he says, "I'll let Jerry know today, and I'll have to start getting things packed."

7

I've been staying over at Daryl and Hunter's place for a couple of days, and fuck it's been a frustrating morning! It's been about six months since I started trying to write this book, and I'm still only at page twenty-one! Sometimes I feel like I'm taking one step forward and four back! I'll write some shit, then read it, hate it, try to change it, and end up writing pretty much the same shit I wrote in the first place!

"AAAAGGH!"

Daryl tells me not to be so impatient, but I can't help it, man. Does this fucking happen to other writers? There must be some trick to it because I just don't get it! I've been told to just write, just get the ideas down on paper and all the editing will come later. And I've tried to do that, but whenever I read what I've written, I'm always trying to fix it. But sometimes, like today, I feel just like chucking the whole fucking thing out the window and forgetting about it!

"Was that you who hollered?" Hunter says entering the room.

"Yeah."

"What's wrong?"

"I'm gettin' fuckin' frustrated writin' this book."

"Nothing's coming out as you'd like it to?"

"Yeah, nothings working out today. I keep fuckin' typing the things from my journals, tryin' to make some kinda story out of it. Then I read it, hate it, throw it out and start it all over. I fuckin' hate days like this!"

"Can I ask you something?"

"Yeah, go for it."

"Why don't you put your writing aside for a moment?"

"Why?"

"You need a break from all this emotion you're putting yourself through."

"Yeah, but I wanna fuckin' write this fuckin' book."

Hunter lights up a joint and passes it to me.

"Here, have a toke and take a break for a bit. I'm gonna make a coffee, do you want one?"

"Sure," I say taking the joint and having a toke.

I pass the jay back to Hunter who has a toke then goes to the kitchen counter and starts making a small pot of coffee.

"So, tell me about your story," Hunter says.

"What's to tell?"

"When did you decide that you wanted to write a book?"

I think about that for a few seconds.

"I guess this whole thing began while I was still in Vancouver Remand Centre waiting for my second trial," I begin. "I got to know a guy named Derek and—"

"Was he cute?" Hunter asks.

"Yeah, he was a cute bastard."

"I love bad boys," Hunter grins.

"Me, too," I say. "Anyways, we got along really good. We'd sit and talk a lot, and it was him that told me I should write a book about my life."

"Really?"

"Yeah, I thought he was full of shit when he first said that to me, but after I was sentenced and was transferred from remand to jail, I got thinking about it, and thought it was worth a try."

"What was it that changed your mind?"

"I really had it with life inside. I was fucking tired of always being on-guard against some of those pieces of shit who wanted to fight me all the time. *And* I wanted to do something good with the rest of my life!"

"How do you see writing a book as doing something good?"

"What the fuck d'ya mean by that?"

"Maybe that came out wrong," Hunter says. "What I mean is, what are your hopes for this book?"

I shrug. "I'm not sure. I guess I want to tell people to do good shit to other people. Don't hurt other people, especially kids, because you only fuck them up."

"How in the world did you even begin to put a book like that together?" asks Hunter.

I shrug again.

"When I first got out of the slam, I had to keep these daily journals of what was happening with me."

"Why was that?"

"My probation officer, Carol, told me it was so she could assess my mental state at the end of every week."

"Interesting," says Hunter, "I didn't even know they had probation officers inside."

"Yeah, they do."

"And they were concerned about your mental state?"

"I dunno. All I knew was all of us cons had to do it."

"Oh, okay. Please continue," Hunter says.

"So, I kinda got into the writing. Besides the journals, I'd be writing on anything I could get my hands on… old notebooks, scraps of paper, shit I even used toilet paper one time just so I would have something to write on."

Hunter smiles. "So, you've decided to write for a living."

"Yeah… I guess I have. I never thought of that."

"How were you fixed for pens and pencils to write with when you were inside? Because I heard they considered those things weapons."

"Actually, gettin' pens and pencils was no biggie, there was always one lying around somewhere. Y'know, it was like, once I started writing I couldn't stop! Things about my life would just come pouring out of me."

"Wow! Fantastic!" Hunter says. "What happened then?"

"Well, I knew Carole liked to read, so I asked her to read a couple of little stories I wrote about my life, and she agreed to. Then, a couple of days later, she called me into her office and told me she really liked what I wrote. I remember her tellin' me that they added to what my journals were tellin' her."

"I remember her sayin', 'You know, with a little bit of formal training, you could be a damn fine writer.'"

"That's nice to hear," Hunter says.

"Yeah, it was."

"Anyways, she told me that there were high school English courses available to me and wanted to put me in one. I told her that I never been good in school."

"What did she say?"

"I remember she told me that it would really look good for me if I took some of these courses. It would let her know that I was wantin' to improve my life, and it could help me improve my writing skills too."

"And what did you say?"

"I told her I ain't smart enough for it."

"What did she say?"

"She told me that's why I would take this kind of course, to learn *how* to do things like this. She asked me, 'do you want to get out of here in a good way?'"

"And what did you answer?"

"I wasn't sure what she meant. Then, I remember her saying, 'Let me put it this way, you can either just do what you've been doing, but now you're back outside, what now? I remember that I shrugged and said, 'I don't know.'

"Exactly," she said. "Or, you can take this program, then maybe get your GED and have a chance at getting a job, and who knows what kind of opportunities might open for you. Doesn't that sound like a chance worth taking?"

"And you jumped at the chance?" Hunter asked with a smile on his face.

"I guess I did" I said. "I remember her telling me, 'It's up to you Givens, but for once in your life, why don't you make things easier on yourself?'

"I remember thinking about it and saying, 'Sure… okay, let's do it.'"

"So, you started your classes right away?" Hunter asked.

"I was supposed to, but it took me a while, like a week, to finally start showing up at the English classes regularly."

"Why was that?"

"I always hated classes and still do, so Carole was starting to come down hard on me because of the classes I was missing. She started telling me that she would take away some of my privileges unless I started going. It was just like me bein' back in school when I was a kid. But y'know, I kind of got used to going to them classes. The part I liked the best was writin' stories and going to them classes gave me a chance to do that every week."

"So, you got into it, then?"

"Yeah, I went to class, and because of that, Carole told me to go for my GED. I agreed. So, she put me in basic math class and some social studies."

"How did you like going to those classes?"

"They were okay, I guess. Carol told me to study hard, and I finally did what I was told. At the end of all that, I had to do this five-part test, which I fuckin' passed! Fuck, was I ever proud of myself the day I was given that GED Certificate!"

"And you should be proud, that was quite an accomplishment." Hunter smiles handing me a cup of coffee.

I look at him leaning on the counter stirring his cup and then I smile. Him telling me those things, brings back the things I was feeling back then. Having that GED meant that I could put that on a resumé for when I got job hunting.

"So, do you remember the moment when you decided that you wanted to write about your life?" Hunter asks.

I think about that a minute.

"I guess it was about then that I decided that I was going to write this book. So, just as I was startin' ta work with Carole and she had me write them journals when I was back in the community. So, these last two and a half years I been keeping notebooks full of my writing, and just adding to them as I go along! I guess I liked writin' in 'em."

"Yes, I've noticed you've been writing in notebooks just about every day. So, what is your book about?"

"It's about my life. But then, what else would it be about, I guess."

"So, here's an important question," Hunter says. "Why is it important that you put this book together?"

I think about that again.

"Putting this book out is really important to me cuz I've had to fight for everything ever since I was kid. Everywhere I ever turned there was something else I had to fight for. I fought my cousins, I fought my teachers, the Social Services, my foster mom Jenny, and her psychotic family. Then I ended up in jail a couple of times fighting them too. I don't wanna do it no more!"

I pause, then say, "I just want to do somethin' with my life. I wanna be somebody. I know I ain't been the best guy in the world but dammit, I want people to respect me! And I'm feelin' that if I can get this book out, it gives me a chance to leave something good behind, something that people might want to read, so they know who I really am… even though I still don't fucking know."

"That's a great answer!" Hunter says. "And it's a great reason to write a book! Have you thought of a title yet?"

I shrug again. "I guess I haven't got that far yet."

"Any ideas at all?"

I smirk. "Maybe…*Sex, Love and Moving On*."

Hunter raises his eyebrows. "That's got a ring to it."

"Or maybe I can call it, *No Bird Like a Jailbird!*"

Hunter laughs. "Or you could call it *Prison Cell Wet Dreams!*"

I laugh. "Or *There's a File in the Cake!*"

We both giggle.

Then he says, "How about, *Don't Drop the Soap If You Don't Want a Grope!*"

We both laugh.

"*Chain Gang Lust!*" I answer.

We laugh again and start going back and forth.

"Toto, We Ain't in Juvey No More!"

"Goodbye Ass Virginity!"

"The Big Book of Prison Romance."

"Vacation at the Medium Security Hilton."

"Cell Mates and Flatulence."

"The Manly Art of Being a Bad Boy's Bitch!"

"The Joys of Cavity Searches."

"The Prison Kitchen Diarrheas."

"I remember you mentioning to me once that you felt being back in Vancouver was your last chance to make something of your life."

"Yeah, I kinda remember that."

"So, Vancouver's your last chance town."

We both stop suddenly.

"Wow, I fuckin' like that!" I say. "*Last Chance Town*. I'm gonna use it!"

"While you're at it, why don't you make it easy on yourself and lift some of the passages from your journals and put them in your book?"

"I never thought about that."

"They would probably fill up a lot of pages."

"That's a fuckin' great idea! I'll do that!"

"Fantastic! You know what you should do right now?" Hunter asks.

"What?"

"Put what you're doing aside, have another toke, and go out for a walk."

"Why?"

"Because you need some fresh air right now, and you're only going to get more frustrated the longer you sit here trying to write."

"I don't know…"

"Put it away for now," he says. "Have a toke and go outside for a walk. Clear your mind, enjoy just being in the moment for an hour or two. Then come back and continue to write."

"I kinda like that idea."

"I guarantee you'll feel better."

And so, I put my stuff to one corner of the kitchen table, have a toke, and put my shoes on. Then I kiss Hunter. "Thank you."

On my way out the door, I grab my notebook and pen. For some reason, when I walk, I get a lot of ideas to write about. I take a deep breath of the cool air and walk aimlessly on this crisp, gray, fall afternoon. I let my mind wander and after walking a couple of blocks, I find myself at a small city park. I sit on a nearby bench, take out my notebook and pen and start scribbling:

> When we were inside, there was a strong "Con code" among us. We all hated the terms "inmate" and "offender" because they weren't us, that was just straights, suits and screws labelling us. And besides, those words sounded too institutional, not human, we were Cons. I wasn't proud to be one, I didn't wear it like some badge of honour like some of the guys did! But that's what we were. Anyways, the Con code was an understood thing. It's supposed to be all about how we could look out for each other, be in each other's corner when we had to be, be true, be solid, be loyal… and its total bullshit!
>
> All the fuckin' Con code did was fuck with your head. The guys formed little "gangs," and they'd corner you in the showers, rough you up and fuck you to prove who was the Alpha. They'd take anything they wanted from you, money, clothes, cigarettes, whatever, and if you told on anyone who did it to you, you were fucked!
>
> I remember being in the gym one afternoon not long after I started my first beef inside, when I heard something happening on the far side of the gym and around a corner so I couldn't see nothing. I heard a lot of what sounded like some kinda commotion or something. Some guy was yelling,

'FUCK OFF!' Then it sounded like someone put a gag on him. Then came this ungodly yet muffled scream! I was so fuckin' out of there!

No, I didn't see nothin'!

No, I didn't hear nothin'!

And no, I don't know nothin'!

Next thing, there were fully armed guards running by me in the hall and they were heading toward the gym. I made it back to my cell just on time for another fuckin' lockdown. I hated those things because we never knew how long we'd be locked down for. We could be locked down for a half hour, or for a few days! Depended on what fucking happened.

We were lucky that time, the guards unlocked our cells an hour afterwards.

I found out later who the poor fucker was, and that he opened his mouth to the Screws about somethin' he shouldn't have, so he got both his knees capped. Poor fuck-wit didn't learn that there ain't no secrets among the Cons, they'll find out who did what, and that, to me, was what the Con code was all about. Never mind the loyalty shit. It was just a code of silence, of letting the Alphas and their crew get away with as much shit as you'd let them.

Being in the Slam also meant being surrounded by stupid shits, and that goes for the Cons, the Screws, and the Suits. It was always a case of "excuse me, is that your arse or a hole in the ground?" I almost said that to a couple of the Screws and a couple of the Cons, but Gil would get me aside and get me to keep my mouth shut just on time. I knew I would have been royally fucked if I said those things! So, I didn't say nothing thanks to Gil.

But prison life had a couple of good moments too. Some of the guys were good shits, like Gil and Derek. And my probation officer Carol helped me out when everyone else thought I was just another Con. I'll never forget them for all they've done for me. They gave me encouragement when I really needed it, and they cared about me when I thought nobody gave a shit.

8

I've been getting rid of some of my old shit and packing the stuff I wanna keep. I look around the room, and I can't believe how many things I've been taking out of boxes and thinking, why the fuck was I keeping this? Daryl said that I can start moving in anytime, and he's cleared out the bedroom I'll be renting on the main floor, so I've already stored a lot of my stuff over there.

Don's moving over to Jerry's apartment in Kitsilano for now. Kitsilano is yuppie town if there ever was one! Their apartment sounds like a nice place though I've never been there. I guess it's not far from the beach and has a fantastic view of English Bay. I can't stand the area though, too many pretenders. But they like it so that's all that matters. Him and me had a yard sale out the front of the building, and I made $62 so that helps with the move.

I've got my boom box on and tuned into CFOX-FM while I pack. Guns and Roses are playing "Welcome to the Jungle" while I'm going through boxes and the music ricochets off the walls of this near-empty apartment. Ozzy's worried, he's been hanging close by me meowing and wondering what's going on. I put my cigarette in a nearby ashtray and tell him everything's all right. I tell him that we're going somewhere new to live real soon. I don't know whether he understands or not, but he seems to be okay with that.

Then I get distracted by one of the notebooks that I've been making notes in for *Last Chance Town*. Man, the more I think about that title, the more I like it. I reach over for it and open it to something that I wrote a few months ago.

It was Jenny, my foster mom, who told me that mom gave me away because she didn't love me.

At first, I told her she was full of shit. That's when she whapped me across the face with a Bible and made me kneel in the corner and pray to God for forgiveness. She and her husband were religious weirdos and major psychos!

Then, because a long time went by and I never heard from mom, I started believing Jenny. But it still didn't make any sense to me that mom wouldn't love me anymore. It just never made any sense because I always felt like there was something missing. Something that Jenny wasn't telling me. But I didn't have no proof of that.

I remember this one night, after Jenny and her fat slug of a husband locked me in my room for sassing them again. I was feeling really lonely and started remembering things from earlier in my life.

I was remembering times when I was about five or six years old back in Edmonton, and Dad showed up drunk on our doorstep one night yelling that he wanted money. Mom yelled at him through the door to fuck off! He just banged on the door even more. Mom started to phone the police when he barged in and started wailing on her. I hid behind the couch. I was scared as fuck as I heard her screaming as he dragged her to the bedroom to beat her. Fuck, I wanted to cry and scream, but that meant he would know where I was hiding.

I held it all in while he was yelling shit at her like, "It's all your fuckin' fault I didn't make much of my life, you bitch! You and that fuckin' son of yours!"

"He's your son too!" she yelled back, then screamed again as he beat her and called her a whore.

Then he came out of the bedroom looking for me. "Where the fuck are ya? You little good-for-nothin' half-breed! I'll beat yuz to a fuckin pulp!"

That's when he pulled the couch back and found me. He picked me up by the collar and I started screaming. That's when Mom ran up behind him and pushed him so hard that he fell and his head hit on the coffee table. He was laying still.

Mom took me and left the house. She was still bloodied and crying, in fact, I remember we were both crying as she was getting me ready to go. She was hurting, and afraid that she might have killed the fucker. We just had the clothes we were wearing, no time to pack nothing, just got the fuck out of there! We went over to a neighbour's place where she called the cops who came and got us and took us to this shelter.

The fucker didn't die because he somehow found out where we were and there were a couple of times that he tried to get at us while we were at the shelter. But the staff and the cops wouldn't let him anywhere near us, thank Christ.

We eventually moved in with Kookum, and the next thing I know I'm being hunted down by those social workers and cops at school, and I never saw Mom or Kookum again.

That was back in the late 1960s, and since then I found out that because my mom was Cree and her marriage broke down, the government went in and took the kids from Native people back then… never from white folks. They were looking for any excuse to take native or half-breed kids away.

And because they were taking away so many kids from their families, the government was having a tough time placing them in permanent white homes. They were desperate, and that's how I ended up being placed with Jenny and her fucking religious whackjobs!

What a bunch of fucking psychopaths! "Full of Praise the Lord" and "ain't we so damn good!" But she was the meanest bitch ever! She always beat on us kids, there were three of us, and I lost it on her a few times. I hit her back when she hit me and then she'd really lose it and start beating me with a belt, calling me a "heathen half-breed" or "the Devil's spawn" and whatever other shit she could fling at me. I hated her and that husband of hers. All he did was sit in a recliner chair all day watching TV. I told them I hated them as much as I could too. I ran away a few times, but the cops would always bring me back to them. Then I'd really catch shit!

This went on for…I can't even remember how long. Then, when I was about eleven or twelve years old, Jenny and me got into it again, and she hauled me in front of Pastor Ormand at their church. I'll never forget that day as long as I live. I remember that whole scene just like it was last week.

Jenny must have been talking to Pastor Ormand about all the trouble I was causing her because the first thing he did was say, "You just can't keep out of trouble, can you, you dirty half-breed?"

I didn't say nothing.

"You know what God does to children like you?"

I didn't say nothing, but I was already pissed off, and he was making me madder!

"He sends the likes of dirty, wicked kids like you straight to Hell!"

Then he started raising his voice. "Is that what you want? Well, it's what dirty, half-breeds like you deserve!"

I couldn't take it no more. "OH YEAH? TALK ABOUT DIRTY! I HEARD THAT SOME FOLKS AROUND HERE ARE SAYIN' THAT YOU'RE DIDDLIN' LITTLE GIRLS!"

Jenny gasped.

His eyes widened, his face got red, he flew into a rage. Storming over and grabbing me by the shirt he started shaking and hitting me. He was screaming at the top of his lungs. "YOU GODDAMNED LITTLE LIAR!"

He threw me on the ground.

"WHO TOLD YOU THAT? HOW DARE YOU BRING YOUR FILTHY MOUTH INTO THE HOUSE OF THE LORD!"

He shook me even harder and had his hands around my throat. He was squeezing hard! I couldn't breathe, I couldn't say nothing! I was trying to break his grip from my throat!

Jenny started yelling at him. "PASTOR ORMAND! PASTOR ORMAND! STOP IT! STOP IT!"

He wouldn't.

"WHO TOLD YOU THAT? BY THE LORD GOD ALMIGHTY, I'LL KILL YOU, YOU LYING LITTLE HALF-BREED BASTARD! YOU'RE BETTER OFF DEAD ANYWAY YOU GODDAMNED LITTLE LIAR! GOD HATES YOU!"

Jenny was still yelling. "PASTOR ORMAND! PLEASE STOP! HE'S JUST A LITTLE BOY!"

For the first time ever, I could hear fear in her voice.

Then she somehow wrestled me away from him, and it sounded like she was sobbing.

I fucked off away from her, and out of his reach choking and crying.

It was like he slowly realized that he lost control of himself. He got this shocked look, and his face went real pale. Then he almost ran toward the altar. He stopped, turned around and looked like he was real scared.

"Jenny," he said as his voice cracked, "please don't bring him in here again. He's irredeemable."

That's when I ran out of the church, and from their grip.

This time, I was gonna make sure I wasn't going to be taken back to any of them. I was gonna stay out of sight of them for good. Fuckers! I hope they're all fucking dead!

The phone rings and startles me! I put Ozzy on the floor to answer.

"Hello."

"Warren, my man!"

"Hey Daryl! What's up?"

"You think you can be ready to move the rest of your stuff tomorrow?"

"Shit. Wasn't countin' on bein' moved that fast, why?"

"My friend with the truck has some time tomorrow if you're ready to go then, for a nominal fee."

"What kind of nominal fee we talkin' about?"

"Fifty bucks."

"Seriously? That's all?"

He chuckles. "Okay, I'll ask him if he wants to charge you more then."

"Yeah, alright. I'll be ready for tomorrow then. What time's he thinkin' of arriving?"

"Say, nine in the morning? You got a lot of stuff to move yet?"

"Big stuff like my stereo, bed, and some other furniture and a few more boxes. All my small shit's already over there."

"Okay, tell you what, I'll come over with him and between the three of us, we can have you moved over here by early afternoon."

"I like the sounds of that."

"Okay. See you tomorrow morning then."

"Yeah, see you at nine."

I look around the apartment and think, fuck, I've got my work cut out for me.

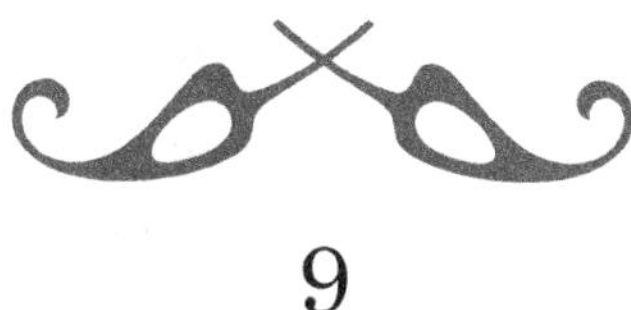

9

There was a commotion going on outside, and it was sounding pretty serious. I glanced at my clock radio, and it was 2:34 AM. I looked out the window to an empty cab in the middle of the street and a guy chasing another guy wearing a turban around the car with a knife!

"HOLY SHIT!" I yelled.

Daryl gave a startled jump. "What?"

"There's a guy with a knife chasin' another guy outside!"

There was a phone by our bed, so I dialed 9-1-1 right away, all the while keeping an eye on the action outside. I told the woman who answered what was happening while the guy with the knife was yelling. "I'll kill ya, you fuckin' foreigner!"

"The cabbie's trying to keep his distance," I said. "He's trying to stay on the opposite side of the car from the guy with the knife."

"What is your address?" The woman asked. I no sooner told her than I heard sirens and saw three cop cars, lights flashing and sirens going, squeal on to the scene right away!

"Wow, that was quick," I said. "The cops are here already!"

"Yes." She sounded amused. "We've had other calls about this incident. Now I just need to know your name."

"Ah…" I hesitated, not trusting anything that has to do with uniforms. "It's Warren."

"Okay thank you, Warren," she said. "Are you at…" and then she told me this address.

"Uh, yeah. How did you know that?"

"It appears on our monitor with your phone number. We'll follow up with you in a little bit."

Meanwhile, I watched as the guy with the knife run on to our lawn and down the side of our house, through the backyard and disappeared into the alley. A couple of other cop cars pulled up and the cops on the scene ran down our side yard to the back. I notice a couple of others run down a side street, I guess to head-him-off-at-the-pass.

I was all keyed up and went down to the kitchen to get a drink of something, anything! Daryl joined me in the kitchen.

"You okay?"

"Yeah," I said takin' a gulp of milk. "Shit like this fuckin' scares me cuz it reminds me of my time inside."

"I hear ya," Daryl answered.

Then a knock came to the front door and Daryl answered it.

"Warren," Daryl said, "it's for you."

I went to the front door to see this cute cop waiting in the front hall. He was short, had a beautiful moustache, brown eyes, and a warm smile.

"Warren?" The cop asked.

I nodded.

"I just need to ask you a few quick questions about what you saw."

I was fuckin' freaked inside, but I answered his few questions and then the cop left. According to him, that whole thing was over a seven-dollar cab fare.

It's been a few months since I've moved in with Daryl and Hunter, and even though I have my own bedroom downstairs, me and Daryl have sleeping together in his room. We've gotten to like each other a lot, and we been getting real close, quick-like. Don't know where this is going to go, but I'm willing to ride this train wherever it takes us. I like him, that much I know.

One thing's for sure, I sure am getting used to the kind of breakfasts that Daryl's been making for me every morning. Like right now I'm chowing down on nice, fat sausages, scrambled eggs with cheese, onions and a bit of salsa, toast, these amazing hash browns with spice and garlic, and the tastiest coffee I've ever had. Man, I'm eating like I haven't had a good breakfast in years! Come to think of it, I can't remember when I've had good breakfasts like these.

"I love these great breakfasts," I say looking at Daryl.

"It's my favourite meal," Daryl says. "Besides, I only cook for guys I like."

"Marry me," I say while smiling and winking at him.

He smiles and winks back.

"It's great that you're the one cookin' in the mornings," I say, "cuz I do enough cooking when I'm at work."

"Hey, I like this song," Daryl says as he gets up to turn up the radio to the Travelling Wilburys' "Handle with Care."

"Yeah, me too. These guys are great. And you know what else?"

"What?"

"I'm really likin' living here," I say.

Ozzy jumps up on one of the kitchen chairs and roars a meow for attention. We both laugh and pet him.

"But I'm still thinkin' about what happened last night."

"Yeah," he answers, "I suppose we should have called the police but—"

"Hell no, not while I was stoned."

Daryl nods and smiles.

"In the years that I've lived in this house nothing like that's ever happened before. Maybe it was new tenants in the apartment building across the alley, who clued in that we're gay."

You see, last night we were just getting settled in to watching TV, when we heard something in the kitchen sound like a small glass breaking, *Clink! Clink!* We came out to the kitchen and were looking around when we noticed small shards of glass around the sink. Then we noticed the small holes in the upper part of the kitchen window.

We checked to see where they might have come from. Daryl said that for the shots to punch small holes like that they couldn't have been at much of an angle. With the fence behind the house, that left the apartment building across the alley. Some asshole decided to take a couple of shots at our kitchen window with a pellet gun or an air rifle. At first, we didn't know if this is because we're gay or what. Then we decided it was a couple of the drunk, local yahoos taking random potshots at the neighbours.

Later, Hunter called us in to his bedroom at the back of the house where he showed us two more pellet holes in the window. Now we're wondering if this really was done to put a scare into us.

It's then that Hunter slides into the kitchen in his underwear and socks, stopping at the kitchen counter and twirling around a couple of times.

"Good morning, all," he sings as he pours some coffee into his thermos. "How are my two good roomies today?"

"Just talking about last night," says Daryl.

"Oh, the windows," says Hunter. "It's a shame there are such angry people in the world. They really have to take a good laxative, drink a couple of hot cups of coffee, then go to the bathroom and let it all go."

Daryl and me look at each other.

He says, "I don't know what to do with that remark."

"Me neither." I shrug and continue eating.

"And what are you fine gents up to today?" Hunter asks.

"I have to go to rehearsal soon," Daryl says.

"And I'll be going to work in about an hour," I say. "How about you?"

"I have the day off today. All kinds of time to get into all kinds of trouble," he says as he tightens the lid on his thermos and dances around the kitchen with it.

"If Lauren Bacall phones," Hunter says as he twirls around the room, "please tell her that I *am* available for lunch in Paris today after all." Then he slides out of the kitchen and goes back upstairs.

We look at each other and quietly smile.

"He's weird," says Daryl, "but he's fun."

10

"Gaaaary! Open the fuckin' door!"

Ah shit, not again.

"Gaaaary! Open the fuckin' door!"

We went through this shit last month, and the month before that!

"Gaaaary! Open the fuckin' door!"

I'm really beginning to hate Welfare Wednesdays.

"Gaaaary..."

Enough of this shit!

I get out of bed and yell out the window, "Gary, open the fuckin' door so the rest of the goddamned neighbourhood can get some fuckin' sleep!"

Daryl stirs in the bed.

The drunk older woman on the back porch looks up at me. "Mind yer own business, ya fuckin' goof!"

I slam the window shut and sit back down on my side of the bed. By this time, Daryl is awake.

"That bunch next door are crazy-assed bastards!" I mumble. "Ya never hear a fuckin' peep from them all month, until Welfare Wednesday, then they party like fuckin' crazy till the money's gone. Last month she was yelling that same thing, but she was up on the fuckin' roof!"

"MmmHmm," says a groggy Daryl.

"How the hell she got up there I'll never know! The fire department had to come and fuckin' get her down."

"I know, I was here, remember?" Daryl yawns.

I fall back and my head thuds into the pillow. Daryl chuckles and puts his arm around me.

"What's so fuckin' funny?"

"You, getting all bent out of shape over the drunken old lady next door."

"Well, yeah I'm pissed cuz she's keepin' me awake, and I gotta work in the mornin'!"

He stops smiling and looks at me seriously.

"Y'know what?"

"What?"

I gotta admit that I'm a little nervous because it felt like there was something he wanted to tell me last night, but we got fuckin' around, and he didn't get around to it. So, like now I'm waiting for the shoe to drop.

"You've probably noticed that I'm not calling you Givens lately."

I think about that. "Yeah, I have. Why?"

"Calling you Givens is impersonal. It's not you."

"It's my name though."

"Sure, it's your last name, but it's not the name your parents gave to you."

I do a double take because I'd never thought about that. "Guess I just got used to it when I was inside."

"But you're not inside anymore. In fact, how long has it been since you've been outside?"

"Two and a half years."

"When I was in juvey, I was told the reason that they called us by our last names was to rob us of our individuality. You've been out for a while now. It's time to reclaim who you are."

I'm silent as I think about that for a sec. I turn and silently look at him. He smiles.

"I'm giving you your name back, Warren."

Hearing somebody call me by my first name jolts me. I haven't heard that for years. I don't know what to say. I smile, kiss him, and snuggle up against him.

"I'm so lucky to have someone like you."

11

The news guy on the radio sounds fully caffeinated this morning. Daylight streams through the kitchen window, making the dirty dishes on the counter even dirtier than they are. I yawn while I sip my own coffee, hoping to find some energy.

> *In the news this morning, we look in on how the final preparations are going for the 1988 Olympic Games which will be held later this year in Calgary, Alberta. Our reporter is standing by to fill us in…*

I thought living in the West End was crazy, but it was a different crazy than what I'm living here. I lived downtown, I worked downtown, and I played downtown. They were crazy times, and I smile to think about it.

You know what though? Living in East Vancouver is even more crazy! Like we still don't know who put the pellet holes through the kitchen window, or why. Then the noisy drunks next door.

> *Meanwhile, The United States Supreme Court overturns a lower court decision to award Televangelist Jerry Falwell $200,000 for defamation against Hustler Magazine…*

Yesterday, I was walking home from work and was coming up Clark Drive. Then from out of nowhere, this car screeches out of the alley on the opposite side of the street, speeds across Clark Drive right in front of me, heading west down the alley. Two cop cars—lights flashing and sirens going—were chasing him! As fast as it started, it ended. But then the air was full of the sounds of sirens, like they were all around me! I got spooked and just wanted to get home.

I take another sip of my coffee.

> *And finally, a three-judge panel of 9th US Circuit Court of Appeals in San Francisco Strikes down the Army's ban on homosexuals…*

What was that I just heard on the radio? Ah fuck, I was so deep in thought that I missed it, oh well…

"Beds are Burning" by Midnight Oil comes on the radio, and I got a strange feeling while I was writing some stuff for my book again last night. I guess it reminded me of where I came from. I don't know why I want to be reminded of that, because most of my life ain't been so great to think about. But you know, that's the whole reason I want to put all the shit I went through into a book.

Carole used to remind me of that whenever I'd get down about a mark I got in class or some shit.

Whenever I would meet with her, I'd be like, "I'm tryin' but I don't feel like I'm nowheres."

"'Well, you can congratulate yourself on where you've come *from*. You've made a lot of progress. Be proud of that, even if it doesn't feel like you're getting anywhere, the fact that you're in class right now trying to build a solid plan for when you go back to the community shows me that you're getting serious about your life. Keep on, keeping on. Baby steps. You'll get there, just keep trying. Don't give up.'"

"But I still landed back in jail," I said.

"'Only so you can learn some manners,' she said, 'and how to organize your life better.'"

I remember that last bit felt like I got hit upside the head with a cast iron skillet. I remember that was the thing that really kicked my ass good. From that point forward, I hit the books pretty hard. Just the idea of *organizing my life better* was just what I needed to hear.

I'm interrupted by Hunter coming into the kitchen.

"Good morning."

I look up and he's smiling at me.

"Hey." I close my notebook.

"Did you sleep well?" He asks grabbing two mugs and draining the coffee from the pot into them.

"Humph," I grunt. "I was having dreams about my past."

"That a good or bad thing?"

"Not good."

"Sorry to hear that."

"Not a big deal." I look at the two mugs. "You had company last night?"

"Yeah, Auntie Vivian came in from Portland late last night."

Auntie Vivian's real name is Rory, and him and Hunter have been friends for-fuckin'-ever. He's a bearded, chubby teddy bear who's fun to be with. He's stayed with us a couple of times when he's been up here before.

He's the lead singer of a Portland electro/punk band called the Romanian Slut Sisters. He says they got the name from some old porn film. They dress in radical drag when they perform, and they've had a single called "Up Your Ass!" that was popular on the college radio stations about a year back. They're popular at gay events down there.

"Did I know he was coming?" I ask wondering if I'd forgotten he was going to be here.

"Yep."

"Oh. Okay."

Just then, Auntie Vivian appears in the kitchen doorway. "Taa-daaaa!" He sings loudly as he enters the room with his arms outstretched to the ceiling. "Stand back girls, I feel a nelly spell coming on!"

Hunter shrieks in delight.

"Didja miss your Auntie Vivian, Tina?"

He always calls me Tina. I don't know why, and I don't *wanna* know why. I smile.

"Yep."

"Good. Now Hunter, what worlds are we going to conquer today?" And he takes the coffee cup that Hunter gives him.

"There's good shopping downtown," says Hunter, "and then lunch, a movie and then the Castle for drinks after that."

"OH FUN!" exclaims Auntie Vivian. "You coming, Tina?"

"No, I gotta work this afternoon."

"Maybe you can join us at the Castle later then."

"Sure, that'll work."

"Meanwhile," Auntie Vivian says, "my sister Hunterina and me are going downtown! Have you got your whorehouse red square dance skirt ready, darling?"

"I've been starching crinolines all week," Hunter answers.

"AHHHHHH!" Auntie Vivian shrieks. "We're going to scare the hell out of Vancouverites this afternoon!"

I can only imagine how they're going to make sure that *everybody* knows that they're there.

12

The Castle is hosting its usual standing-room-only Saturday afternoon crowd. With the packed crowd, it's fucking boiling in here, and the heat and B.O. are starting to get to me a bit. I'm sitting at the table with Hunter, Auntie Vivian, and three of their friends.

Work was okay today. I found out that I've been given a raise starting with my next paycheque, so that's bonus! I can sure use the extra money.

Uh oh, Auntie Vivian has his shirt off and entertaining everyone as he stands up, puts his arms out to either side of him like a cross, and starts to shake so his chubbiness jiggles. He calls it his Jesus Jelly Mold. Everyone laughs.

I look around the crowded room, and there are some real hot guys here this afternoon. But I gotta keep it in my pants tonight because Daryl will be joining us soon. On the other hand, maybe I can talk him into a threesome with one of these hot gentlemen. Then I hear Auntie Vivian's voice above the noise.

"Isn't that right, Tina?"

It feels like I'm slapped back to Earth. "Isn't *what* right?"

"Vancouver's hosting the Gay Olympics in a couple of years."

"We are?"

Everyone at the table laughs.

"I think Warren was distracted by the good-looking guys around us." Hunter smiles. "That's okay, I don't think the fact that the games are coming here has sunk in with most of the gay kids in Vancouver just yet."

"Oh, that's okay," Auntie Vivian says, "it's still a coupla years away yet." Then he starts singing along to Steve Winwood's "Higher Love" now playing on the jukebox.

"Hey!" says a voice over my shoulder. I turn to see a great-looking, bearded guy with glasses smiling at me.

"Hey," I say, "ain't you that new bassist in Hamstring?"

This is the name of Daryl's new band.

"Yep. I'm Kelly. We've met before."

"Really?"

"It was at that party at Drew and Luka's place about a couple of months ago, and we talked about music for a couple of hours."

"Yeah, that's right. I remember now. I guess I was really stoned and couldn't place ya at first."

"That's okay," he says. "Been there a few times myself."

"How ya doing?"

"Great," he says.

"If I remember right, you have a boyfriend, don't you?"

"Yeah, Gord! He should be by in a couple of minutes. Do you mind if we join you guys?"

"No, we don't mind. Let's see if there's any spare chairs around."

Kelly scores an empty chair and pulls it as close to the table he can. I introduce him to everyone.

"So, what's been happening," Kelly asks me.

"Just chillin' after work today."

"I see you've got a new album," he says pointing at the plastic record bag by my side.

"Yeah, I got *Kick* by INXS."

"Aren't they a fuckin' fantastic band?" Kelly says as his face brightens even more.

"Yeah, my last roommate Don really liked them and had all their albums."

That's when our conversation turns to music, about the bands we like, favourite albums, and the music scene in general. The more we talk, the more excited Kelly gets… just like the first time I remember meeting him.

"You and me should go record huntin' someday," he says.

"I'd like that. You busy next Saturday?"

"No. Do you wanna meet up for a munch, then go look at some music."

"That sounds like a plan," I answer.

Just then one of those drunk old bitches up sitting at the bar yells out, "MY WALLET! ONE OF YOUS FAGGOTS STOLE MY WALLET!"

Auntie Vivian yells back. "OH, TAKE A PILL, MARGE!"

He gives Auntie Vivian the evil eye while everyone around us laughs.

That's when Kelly waves at someone, and another big handsome bear comes over to join us.

"You're finally here," Kelly says then turns to me. "You remember him?"

"Yeah, I remember. How ya doin' Gord?"

We shake hands.

"You're Warren, right?"

"Hey, good memory," I answer.

That same old queen is causing a ruckus at the bar now.

"ONE OF YOUS FUCKIN' FAGGOTS STOLE MY WALLET!"

Terry the manager, who's standing nearby, picks the guy's wallet off the floor. "CALM THE FUCK DOWN, DORIS!"

Everybody laughs again.

"LOOK AT THIS!" he says to the guy as he puts the wallet in his hand. "IT FELL OUT OF YOUR POCKET ON TO THE FLOOR!"

More laughter from the crowd as the guy spins around on his stool and leaves the pub in a huff.

Auntie Vivian chuckles and yells as the guy storms out the door. "GAWD! WHAT A DRAMA QUEEN!"

13

I don't know what fuck's going on with me these last couple of weeks. I'm getting winded anytime I go up the stairs. This morning, I haven't even made it all the way up before I've had to sit down and catch my breath. It's weirding me out!

Hunter appears at the top of the stairs.

"What are you doing sitting in the middle of the staircase?"

"I ain't feelin' good."

"Sorry to hear that. What's wrong?" he says as he comes down.

I tell him what's been going on with me.

"How long has this been happening?"

"A couple of weeks."

"Any other things going on physically?" he asks, sitting beside me.

"Well, lately I've been getting these pains in my joints, my head feels real warm, and there's a swelling in my throat just under my jaws that ain't going away."

Silence.

"I guess I gotta quit smoking and cut down going to the bar," I say.

"You're probably right about the smoking thing," he says. "But the pain you're getting doesn't sound right to me. Why don't we make an appointment for you to go to my doctor for a checkup?"

I think about that a sec. I don't like doctors because, like the cops, they don't bring nothing but bad news.

"Ahhh, I don't know..."

"C'mon, don't play around with your health," says Hunter. "Wouldn't you rather know what's happening? And besides, my doctor is really good."

I think again. He's right, this whole thing is too weird.

"Well, okay, let's do it."

14

Hunter's doctor, Dr. Chu, was good enough to get me in to talk to him. I told him what's been happening, and he agreed that I have to quit smoking, but that wasn't the end of it.

"I assume like Hunter, you're gay?"

"Yeah, so what?"

"Well just to rule out any possibilities, I'm sending you for an HIV test."

"You saying you think I might have HIV?"

"No, Warren. What I'm saying is that we want to rule *out* that possibility. The symptoms of HIV are similar to symptoms of other illnesses too. So, the only way to know for sure whether you have been exposed to HIV or not, is to be tested."

"But d'ya think it still might be a possibility?"

He sighs. Nods. "Yes. What you describe and given the way things are in the gay community these days, I think it's a possibility. But we won't know for sure until we get the test results."

"What kinda symptoms we talking about?"

"Well, some of the symptoms are flu-like, and we're talking about things like feeling weak, joint pain, fever, swollen glands, diarrhea, and night sweats. Have you had any night sweats?"

"No, nothin' like that."

Dr. Chu shakes his head a little. "Right, well, this is why I want to test you so we can hopefully eliminate the possibility that you are HIV positive."

All this talk is spooking me.

I don't know what to say, I feel numb and want to say something, but I can't because a rush of fear goes through me.

"You know," says Dr. Chu, "on other hand, the tests might come back negative, and that's a good thing. There's strength in knowing."

Like everything else in my life, I say, "Okay, fuck it, let's do it then."

15

Before I left for the doctor's appointment today, Daryl asked me to meet him at the gay pub at the Dufferin Hotel, when I was done. So that's where I'm heading.

I'm not sure what I'm feeling as I'm walking down Nelson Street toward Seymour Street. The thought that the doctor even wants to eliminate the possibility of HIV scares the fuck out of me. Fuck! What if the results come back positive? I know the doctor told me about false positives, still… On my way, I see two cops talking to a shabby, young street guy. His dirty blue sleeping bag is a messy heap on the sidewalk and he's crying and pleading with the cops. "Please, I don't wanna go to the hospital. Please, please, don't send me to the hospital."

"Too late for that now," one of the cops says while the other one is talking into the mouthpiece pinned on the collar of his coat.

The young guy's still pleading with the cops as I walk by. Why don't they leave that poor bastard alone? It reminds me too much of when the cops and social services came after me when I was a kid—they wouldn't listen to me then, either. Poor guy. Fuckin' uniforms!

I get to Streets and say hi to Cary the manager as he stands behind the bar. I order a pint. Cary serves it up, and I sit at one of the tables. I watch as a shabby bum comes in off the street. He's looking like he's floating on air, right into the washroom. Then I look around the room at the TV monitors flashing music videos. I can just barely hear the sound because it's turned low, but I watch while INXS is playing "Devil Inside". I've seen this video before, and I really like this song. It's from *Kick*, an album I bought a little while ago.

I look at the way this place is decorated. Walking into this pub is like walking down a street with fake storefronts and lighting. The dance floor has two stone lions on either side of it. There's a mural on the wall behind the lions of the south entrance to the Lions Gate Bridge.

There's loud music coming from the Back-Alley Pub which is downstairs and at the back of the building. I hear some guy over a PA system.

"Let's give a big hand for John!" There is cheering. Sounds like a fuckin' great party. *"Next up is Davey! C'mon let's give Davey a big hand!"*

I sip my drink, and I'm in deep thought. *HIV! FUCK!* I realize that if this test comes back positive, I might die soon—and I ain't never even had a chance to live! It's then I realize that, if I'm gonna write my book, I better get my ass in gear! Because I don't know how much time I got left.

That bum comes out of the washroom and leaves the pub, just as I watch a young guy come out of the hotel lobby and go into the washroom. He almost runs out right away, looks at me, holds his nose as he points at the washroom. "Fuckin' brutal!" Then walks back into the lobby. I manage a grin.

That's when I see Daryl come through the front door. He approaches the table and stops cold.

I look at him and I want to cry.

"Okay, I don't like that look on your face," he says as he sits beside me. "What happened at the doctor?"

"He's sending me for some tests."

"What kind?"

I'm silent.

"It's serious then?"

"He thinks I might have HIV."

"Holy shit!"

"The doctor says it's a routine test and it should be okay. But..."

I feel tears running down my face.

"When will you know for sure?" Daryl asks as he puts his hand on mine.

"It'll take three weeks. They'll phone me with the results."

We're silent again. Then Daryl moves closer to me and puts his arm around me.

More silence as he looks to be searching for words.

"This means you'll have to get tested too," I say.

He looks at me, nods. "That's true." His voice is quiet. "I'll make an appointment with the doctor this week."

"You know," Daryl says, "there are such things as false positives."

"That's what Dr. Chu said. He told me he'd send me for another test if it came back positive because of that reason."

"That's become a pretty standard procedure these days," Daryl says.

We hear another cheer go up from the audience down in the Back-Alley Pub.

"I'm scared. I don't want this. I know I haven't been the best guy on earth, but I…"

Daryl kisses me and holds me close to him.

"Don't even *think* about going down that road," he says. "You're perfectly fine exactly as you are."

"Then why is this happening to me? Why was I taken from my family? I've been in trouble all my life. I went to jail twice, and now this. Why?"

"Do you really think you deserve this?" Daryl asks.

"I don't know." I shrug. "If there is a God, why do I feel like He hates me?"

More cheers go up from the pub downstairs, and we both look over where they came from.

"*If* there is a God," he says, "I'm sure He doesn't hate you."

I silently shrug.

The two of us are silent again.

"That sounds like quite a party going on down there," I say trying to lighten things up while wiping the tears with my sleeve.

"Yeah, it does," Daryl smirks.

We're silent for a little bit then Daryl says, "I think there's an amateur strip contest going on down there. Wanna check it out?"

I shrug. "I dunno."

"C'mon, it could be good for a laugh. I think we could both use a good laugh right now."

"I guess you're right, I could use some cheering up right now."

We take our drinks and head down a small flight of stairs and open a pair of double doors to the Back-Alley Pub. The first thing I see is a skinny older guy on the stage, which is more like a small platform. He looks like he might have been good looking back in the day, and except for a pair of shoes and black socks he's totally naked.

He smiles at one guy in the audience in particular as he does his version of the Twist.

"Okay," says the MC into his mic, "okay everyone give a big hand to Davey!"

The crowd claps, whistles, and cheers while Davey picks up his clothes and gets down from the stage. When the cheers die down the MC points to someone in the crowd.

"Up next, we have Mark! Everyone put your hands together for Mark!"

The music starts playing while we all clap. I can see a guy with a bushy beard, potbelly, and lumberjack shirt try to get out of his chair and slip back down. Then he pushes himself up and staggers up to the stage, barely able to climb up. He hardly knows what he's doing as he sort of staggers and shuffles around the small platform trying to move to the music.

Mark lifts one foot to take off his shoe, and misses. He tries again to take it off when he falls sideways into the audience. The audience gasps. But luckily, some of the audience members have grabbed him just on time and have put him back up on the platform.

"Oh, this is gonna to be good." Daryl giggles, and I can feel a smile on my face.

There's no damage as Mark waves to the folks who put him back up on stage. He continues grabbing at his shoe, yanking it off his foot as it flies into the audience. His foot falls with a thud to the stage floor and we start giggling. Daryl puts his arm around my shoulder and I'm likin' it. Meantime, Mark's somehow managed to undo his pants. Then, as he tries to take off the other shoe, his pants fall to the floor, and he rips a loud fart. The audience laughs out loud and cheers while Daryl leans over and puts his head against mine while we laugh.

"Whoa, Mark," says the MC, "you'd better check your underwear!"

Mark waves in the MC's direction just as two bouncers go up to the stage and help Mark off. Which doesn't look to be easy while his pants are down around his ankles and he's too drunk to know up from down. But they manage to get him off the stage while he rips another loud fart. One of the bouncers turns to the audience and puts two of his fingers over his nose while he screws up his face. By this time, Daryl and me are splitting a gut.

"Everybody give a big hand to Mark for an act that mere words can't describe!" the MC laughs as the crowd cheers and gives him a standing ovation.

"I can't take this anymore," says Daryl still laughing. "Let's go back home."

16

The Downtown Eastside. I never like being in this part of town. Drunks, junkies, cheap beer joints, flop houses, bedbugs, cockroaches, desperate people who live desperate lives all find their way to Vancouver's skid row. We're on our way to see Daryl's friend Tony Wells. They've known each other for years. They became friends almost as soon as Daryl arrived in Canada from California. He's always been Daryl's pot dealer. We're going to his place so Daryl can buy some, and he says that Tony wants to meet me.

I look around at the people here, and I remember something that Jenny would always mumble when she'd see someone down-and-out. *There but for the Grace of God go I.* Come to think of it, she used to say that a lot.

We approach the corner of East Hastings and Gore, and I can hear a commotion. We see an animated woman, maybe in her early thirties, screaming and yelling at somebody.

She's naked. And she screams as she throws something at two police officers, standing on the sidewalk, silently looking at her through dark sunglasses. She has a ratty old comforter in her arms as she walks out to the middle of East Hastings Street and plunks it down on the pavement. Then sits on it—right in the middle of the street!

Daryl smiles and leans in. "It's never a good idea to mix your drugs."

I chuckle, but inside I'm thinking, *fuck, that could be me.*

"You're fuckin' losers," she yells at the uniforms while giving them the old trucker's salute. "Ya hear? LOSERS! LOOOSERS!"

Then she stops and digs around the comforter like she's looking for something all the while swearing at the uniforms.

That's when one of the uniforms walks to the middle of the street near her, but just out of her reach in case she gets violent. He talks into the microphone pinned to his collar, then directs traffic around her. The uniform on the sidewalk never takes his eyes off her as he moves in closer to her.

She flips them the bird and continues to dig around in her comforter. We walk by, turn off East Hastings and zigzag for a couple of blocks until we reach an old two-storey apartment building. This old wooden fire trap looks like it's ready to fall down. Old paint chips flake around all the cracks in the building's siding, and someone on the first floor has got a *Dark Side of the Moon* flag strung across their living room window. Meantime, from what I can see of the roof, it's heavy with moss. Somebody's tried to grow some flowers out the front of the place, but let the weeds grow around them and now it looks like shit.

I can't tell when it was last painted, but it looks like it was a hundred years ago. A couple of the windows are broken. One is boarded up. Half a rusted drainpipe is hanging from one corner of the building. I've lived in some dives, but not like this. Daryl pushes the buzzer. No answer, but the door buzzes and we go in.

The lighting in this hallway is dim with a couple of the bulbs burnt out, and the smell is a mixture of cat piss, burnt bitter coffee, cigarette smoke, pot, and moldy old carpet. The walls look like they were painted the same time as the outside. The sound of two women screaming at each other in front of a live audience on one of those stupid afternoon TV shows is coming from somewhere behind one of these doors. We walk down the hallway till we reach a door with 1-D stickered to it. Daryl knocks.

The door opens, and this scruffy old fucker looks at the two of us.

"Kellerman! You get uglier every time I look at ya!"

"You're no prize-winner yourself, Wells."

Then Tony looks at me. "Who the hell are you?"

"Warren," I say extending my hand.

"Oh yeah," he grunts. "Get the hell in here before the neighbours see the both of yous! I can't afford ta lose any more friends!" Then he walks into the apartment.

"What a grouchy old bastard," I whisper to Daryl as we enter to the smell of dirty old socks, beer, and pot.

"I heard that," he says.

Daryl looks at me and smiles. "You *are* a grouchy old bastard, Wells."

"Fuck off! I suppose yer here for dope."

"It's not the pleasure of your company."

Wells grunts, mumbles something, and waves at us to go away.

I look around the room, the torn blinds on the windows are drawn on this sunny late spring afternoon, so it's dark and he has the living room lamps on. Three empty beer cans are discarded on the coffee table, one of them is crushed. A couple of cockroaches sit on top of a half-eaten piece of pizza beside the cans. Things are strewn around the room, and it looks like it hasn't been cleaned since the last time this building was painted. He's got Much Music on the TV. Robert Palmer sings "Simply Irresistible".

Tony was probably a good-looking bastard back in the day. But he's let himself go big time. His dirty T-shirt is ripped and rises over his potbelly, and he has a missing front tooth. His greasy hair is dishevelled, and he looks and smells like he hasn't had a shower since Christ was a cowboy!

"D'ya want a drink or somethin'?" he barks.

"Sure, what have you got?"

"You can have beer or beer."

"Guess I'll have a beer."

"What about you?" Tony says looking at me.

"I'll just have water."

He looks at me like I've got three heads.

"Water? You'll get sick! Have a goddamn beer! It's better for you than the shit that comes from the tap!"

"I'm not drinkin' right now," I say.

"What the fuck?" He looks over to Daryl. "Where the hell didja find *this* one?"

Daryl shrugs. "Just give him some water like he wants."

Wells grunts, pours me a glass of water then hands it to me. "Why anyone would wanna drink that shit is beyond me."

Daryl laughs.

"You think it's funny, d'ya?" Wells barks.

What a fuckin' turd!

"So, howya been?" Daryl asks him.

"I'm gettin' fuckin' old."

"You're *getting* old?"

"Yeah, fuck you too."

Daryl laughs. "Hey Warren, if you want to know what's goin' on in this part of town, this is the guy to ask. He knows everything that's goin' on down here, don'tcha Gladys?"

"Fuck you."

"Gladys?" I ask.

"Gladys Kravitz, you know, like on *Bewitched*? Abner! Abner!"

"I'll fuckin' Abner you if ya don't shut it," Tony says half grinning. "So, what the fuck have you been up to since I last saw ya Kellerman?"

"You know, the usual."

"Yeah, knowin' you, yer still gettin' stoned then fuckin' yer brains out at the tubs. You're never gonna fuckin' grow up are ya?"

"I hope the fuck not."

"So, are you and this arsehole an item, or what?" Tony asks me.

"Yeah."

"Your taste is in your arse," he says.

"He could do worse," says Daryl taking a sip of his beer. "He could be seeing you."

"Don't push it Kellerman."

Daryl laughs out loud.

"I'll be right fuckin' back," Tony says and leaves the room, returning a few moments later with a plastic Ziploc bag. He gives it to Daryl who gives Tony some cash. He counts it out.

"What, no tip? Who taught ya fuckin' manners?" Tony barks again.

"Yeah, you know all about manners, don'tcha?" Daryl shoots back at Wells. "Besides, the only tip you're gettin' is the head of my dick."

"Yeah, I choke on small fuckin' bones," Tony grumbles.

Daryl lets fly with a loud belly laugh.

Then Tony looks at me. "Are you sure you want to be seen with this arsehole?"

I chuckle.

"You're as bad as him," he says pointing at Daryl again. "Ya dumb fucks deserve each other!"

"Never mind him," Daryl says to me. "He's jealous because he's finally met you, and he wants you now."

I look over to Tony who has a bigger grin on his face and looks like he's searching for something to say.

Daryl laughs out loud and claps his hands. "Am I right? Am I right?"

"You got yer pot now get the fuck out of here," Tony says with that grin still on his face.

"C'mon Warren," Daryl says. "We've got things to do anyway. Thanks for the beer and pot, Wells."

"Yeah, yeah, yeah…" he says, "up your arse."

17

It's a couple of weeks later, a lazy evening as I lay on the couch watching the *Kids in the Hall*. I love that Scott Thompson character Buddy Cole. I know gay guys just like him. Makes me laugh every time I watch it.

I finally met our landlord yesterday. Daryl's right, the guy can't keep his hands off anyone. His name is William, and when Daryl introduced us, he just kept staring at me smiling. Then he starts licking his lips at me. The guy's old enough to be my grandfather, and he was coming on to me real hot and heavy. Then Daryl goes out of the room for a minute, and the guy says, "That's a nice-looking basket you have there…" and starts rubbing my crotch. Fuck!

My thoughts are broken by Daryl as he comes into the living room. "Hey, give Tony a call. There's something he wants to tell you."

"Yeah, he wants to fuck me, and the answer's still no!"

"That's not it. Here's his number, just call him. I think you'll want to talk to him."

He didn't really make a good impression on me, but Daryl thinks he's okay, so I take the number and give him a call.

"Yeah, whaddaya want?" This is how he answers the call.

"Daryl told me to give ya a call."

A pregnant pause.

"Is this Warren?"

"Yeah."

"What didja say yer last name was?"

"Givens."

"Okay, that's interestin'."

"Why?"

"I've heard tell there's been two older women in this area lately asking for somebody named Warren Givens. No one knows who the one woman is. The other one's been seen in this area a coupla times in the last coupla months. Talk has it that these women are from Edmonton. Daryl says that's where yer from."

"Yeah," I say, "but I ain't been there for a few years."

"Daryl says yer half Native."

"Yeah, so what?"

"These two women are Native and say they're lookin' for one of the women's son… named Warren. That you?"

"Could be. But I ain't seen my mom since I was a kid."

"Look, if yer maybe interested in finding out if it could be her, I can do some more diggin' and see what I can find out for ya."

"I don't know about that," I say. "It's been too long."

"Okay, it's up to you."

"Thanks for the offer, though," I tell him.

"No skin off me arse."

18

Sometimes after my lunch shift, I'll head downtown just to see what's shaking. Pacific Centre Mall is right downtown and is always a good bet I'll see something there I like to look at, especially some of the guys' asses. Or sometimes, like today, I'll stop for a coffee somewhere, take out my notebook and write the things that I can remember, the things that really stand out in my mind.

It was only later that day, after I ran away from Pastor Ormand and Jenny, swearing that they'll never find me again, that I was caught by Social Services. But by this time, they transferred me to another set of foster parents. The social workers told the new couple there was a clash of personalities between the old foster parents and me. No fucking shit!

They put all my shit in a green plastic garbage bag, and I went to the new foster parents. I didn't give a shit, I hated Jenny and her husband and was glad to be leaving. The new foster parents lived in a rental complex in North Edmonton. Their names were Dan and Lisa and I liked living with them. They were good folks and treated me like one of their own five kids.

I stayed with them for a few years. Then, when I turned sixteen, I quit going to school cuz had no use for the place. I wanted to start making some money, and I tried to get legit jobs at local fast-food places, I asked if they had openings and filled out applications and finally got on at a local McDonald's.

When I wasn't there, I found my way to the place where the local kids hung out. You know, kids with nowhere else to go. And it was then I got to know Bryce real well. Bryce, now there was one crazy-assed bastard. You know how some guys have it all: good looks, money, clothes, class, great body, brains, great smile and good in bed? That was Bryce.

He fucked off from his parents because he was tired of getting the shit kicked out of him by his old man every time he did something. He hung out over at Boys Town where the guy-whores were waiting for tricks. He always wore his cowboy hat and boots, so some of the guys called him Cowboy. He took wearing that hat and those boots real serious, because he was always getting the choice tricks when he wore them. They really liked the young cowboy fantasy, and he could make shitloads of money. Especially from the rich, old pervs from the oil biz.

One day I said to him, "You're smart and could be anything you want to be and make all kinds of money. Why ya hustlin'?"

"Cuz I'm smart, and I know where the money is," he said. "I'm makin' some pretty cool coin sellin' my dick to the old queers."

"So, those old guys are payin' you to fuck ya?"

"Not even," Bryce said. "Most of 'em give me money so they can suck my cock, take pictures of me, whack off for them, it's good fuckin' cash, and it beats the hell outta workin' at McDonald's!"

"Seriously?"

"Seriously."

I didn't need to think about it. I asked how I could get started hustling and Cowboy said he'd show me the ropes. "Show up here tomorrow night, and we'll start."

The next night when I showed up, he looked me up and down. Then he nods.

"So, here's what happens. Ya just stand here and some guy in a car will drive up. He'll ask you how much you want for him to give you a blow job, or for you to give him one or maybe even to fuck your ass."

"No fuckin' way, man! No one's fuckin' my ass!"

"You wanna make money doin' this?"

"Yeah."

"Then get over it!"

I didn't know what the fuck to say. "Okay, then uh, how much do I charge?"

"Leave that to me," Bryce said, "I'll be lookin' out for ya. Anyone approaches ya, I'll take over. But since ya wanna know it's twenty bucks if they want to suck your cock, thirty if they want you to suck them, and I charge fifty if they want to fuck you. Then there's the other stuff…"

"Hold it, man. You're chargin' people to get it on with me?"

"Let me explain somethin' to ya," Cowboy says. "This might look like easy money and fun, but it ain't. There's a lot of pieces of shit out there who are gonna try to get what they can from you for free. These fuckers want you to give them your ass then leave ya with nothin', and there ain't nothin' you can do. No use goin' to the cops cuz they'll just laugh in your face and tell ya not to waste their time. No use tryin' ta make those pieces of shit pay cuz they'll just fuckin' deny ever bein' with you in the first place."

"I never thought about that," I say.

"Believe me, buddy, I had ta learn the hard way. Let's just say that by me makin' all the arrangements you know that you'll get paid, okay?"

"Howya gonna do that?"

"I got connections. That's all ya need ta know."

"So, what about this other stuff you're talkin' about?"

"Sometimes tricks'll want you to be the meat for a bunch of guys," Bryce says. "That's when you can make a real shitload of money…"

"What d'ya mean the meat for a bunch of guys?"

"Sometimes they'll buy a young guy to get naked for a group of old pervs, and they'll want to put you in a porn or gang bang ya."

Fuck, I didn't like the sound of that, and Cowboy must have picked up on that.

"But you don't have to worry about that right now. Just get the basic shit down, one-on-one fuckin', suckin', the odd naked photo shoot and you'll be fine. And, you'll have to get used to gettin' naked with some real old, ugly fuckers."

Okay. Seemed easy enough to me—and he was right. A couple of months later, I was making decent money gettin' pimped out by Cowboy to older fuckers and married guys. I even got to enjoy it after a while. During the day, I'd sleep in, then at night I would have a shower and go out to turn a few tricks down in Boys Town with my new buddy Bryce and get stoned after. It got to the point where I was his number one boy.

I'd let some old queers suck my dick and before I knew it, I'm making way more coin than working for McDonald's. Why should I slave away for nothing while I can do this for a few hours at night and make serious fuckin' coin?

Bryce would arrange for me to have one-on-ones with a client or threesomes with a couple of tired old queens. We'd get paid to be at private parties where we'd be the naked centre of attention in a room full of old business pervs in town for conventions and shit. I couldn't believe how many of these old queers were married, had kids, were big wigs at their churches, and were paying good money to fuck around with young guys on the side.

When I turned seventeen, I told Dan and Lisa that, since I was working full-time at McDonald's (a lie), Bryce and me were moving into a place together. They really didn't like that idea because they thought I was too young. But they knew they couldn't keep me there either. As I was packing, they said they'd miss me and that I was welcome back there anytime. That kinda made me have second thoughts about leaving.

But I packed my shit anyways, and Bryce and me moved into a small, rundown, three-bedroom house on Edmonton's east side. Carl and Wylie, a couple of hustlers we knew, moved into the third bedroom in the place. They were boyfriends and they worked as a team who sold pot on the side. They didn't do too badly as a sex team, and man, they knew how to grow wicked pot! I think of them sometimes, and I wonder what those fuckers are up to these days.

These guys meant a lot to me, and for the first time in my life, I felt like I was part of something. We were like a family laughing, talking, partying, fucking for cash. We had people coming over at all hours, we'd sell them some shit and pocket the profits. Or we'd be going over to Boys Town and turn a couple of tricks for some quick cash, and sometimes we'd have celebration fucks together.

Carl taught me how to grow my own pot. My bedroom was full of pot plants. When I wasn't turning tricks, I'd pick the leaves, dry them, grind them, package them, and it was a tough row to hoe without some decent grow lights. But eventually I had my own regular customers coming to buy pot from me.

Don't get me wrong, there were some scary times too. I remember this one time I was hanging out with one of my regular tricks—Jason, a married guy with kids. He had a day job he hated, a wife who wouldn't have sex with him, was a small-time coke dealer on the side and a closet cocksucker. This one night we're sitting on a park bench and I'm listening to him complaining about his life, and I notice this car driving slowly up the road almost hugging the curb. Next thing I know I see the driver's window roll down and this handgun comes out of the window and started shooting at us. I ducked and fell on the ground as the car sped off. Lucky this fucker

> was a bad shot, and we didn't get hurt, but man what an adrenaline rush!
>
> That's when Jason came clean that he ripped off a guy a couple of weeks before by using the shit instead of selling it for the guy.
>
> "This was probably just a warning," he said.
>
> I told him sayonara and fucked off. He tried to contact me after that, but I told him to stay the fuck away if he's doing that kind of shit. I didn't want my head blown out of shape because he was being stupid!
>
> Then there was that night the cops showed up and raided our place. They went into my room and found my pot plants, the stuff I'd packaged, and a wad of money. Next thing I know my buddies and me are being loaded into an Edmonton Police truck and taken downtown. They booked me for possession for purposes of trafficking, and I ended up in Juvey for a few months.
>
> That's when all these workers at Juvey said they wanted to help me with any problems at home. Any problems at home… yeah, right. Where the fuck were they when I was always being taken back to Jenny and her bunch of psychos? And no, them bastards at Juvey didn't help me at all. They just kept me there. Fuckers!

I look at the time, and realize I've been here for a couple of hours already! I get my shit together and start walking to the other end of the mall to catch my bus home. As I walk, I pass a bench where a little girl is making loud chicken noises at this older lady who's sitting next to her staring into space.

"Bawk, bawk, bawk," the little girl clucks at the old lady. This other woman sitting on the other side of the little girl yells, "QUIT BAWKIN' AT YOUR GRANDMOTHER!" The kid starts crying, and I keep walking. I hate hearing kids crying.

That's when I see this other lady!

I stop in my tracks because she looks just like my mom, leastways, the way I remember her, only older.

I want to go over and ask her name, but I don't. What the hell would I say to her? *Hi mom, missed you? How's things goin'?* And what if it wasn't her? Then I'd feel like a fuckin' idiot! And what if Jenny was right, and she didn't love me and adopted me out to another family? Although that still doesn't make any sense to me.

When I get back home, I ask Daryl for Well's number again, and I dial.

"Yeaahh, whadja want?"

"Tony?"

"Yeah."

"It's Warren."

"Yeah, I know."

"Hey look, I've changed my mind about you askin' around to see if my mom's in town."

He's silent. I can hear some noise in the background. "Yeaaahh, that's it…"

I don't know how to answer that.

"I saw a lady downtown this afternoon that looks like my mom, only older."

"Hey, careful there, suck, don't scrape."

"Ahhh… did I call at a bad time?"

"I got some young hustler here givin' me a blowjob. Call back later."

"Ah… yeah. I'll do that."

19

It's early Saturday afternoon, and I'm just home from work putting some groceries away when the phone rings.

"Hello?" But there's nothing on the other end.

"Hello…" I say again.

I can hear somebody breathing then a woman's voice. "Is this Warren?"

"Yeah."

"Warren Givens?"

There is something about the voice. Then it hits me.

"Mom?"

She's sobbing.

"I've been searching for you," she says. *"It's been many years."*

I can't believe I'm hearing her voice after all this time.

"What, I mean, well, how did you find me?"

"It wasn't easy. Some people that I was talking to told me a man named Tony knew somebody named Warren Givens, and he knew where to get hold of you."

So, Tony had come through for me.

"I've been looking for you ever since you were taken from me," she says. *"I found some people who said they knew you in Edmonton, and they told me you were in jail and were sent down to Calgary."*

"Yeah," I say quietly, "that was true."

"I was in Calgary looking for you for a couple of years. Then I heard there was a guy in Vancouver with the name Warren Givens. I've made

several trips out here to Vancouver and asked around to see where you might be." She sobs.

Hearing Mom's voice again after all these years makes my body shake, and I can't see because I'm crying. I have to sit down on a nearby chair.

"Mom," I say like a hurt little boy, "I've wanted to see you all these years, but Jenny told me you didn't love me anymore and that was why I was with *her* family."

There's quiet from her end of the phone. Then. *"Who's Jenny?"*

"The social workers put me in with her and her fucked up family after they took me from school that day."

She's crying on the phone.

"That's not true, my son," she sobs. *"I found out that your father complained to the government people that I beat you. Then your kookum and I sent you to school that day and you never returned to us."*

I'm quiet. That sounds *exactly* like something that bastard would have done. I fucking *hate* him. And as for that bitch Jenny, she lied to me all these years. But she was so fucked up that I'm not surprised.

"Please, forgive me," Mom says. *"I didn't even know where you were. I even went to Social Services to see if you were in their care. They told me to go away. Told me that you were in a better situation now."*

There's more sobbing from the other end of the phone.

"I promised myself and the Ancestors that I would find you even if it took the rest of my life."

Then something weird happens to me. It's like I can hear a voice speaking in my ears, Kookum's voice, just like I remember it. She's talking to me.

Go and see her, my Little Muskwa, she is your mother.

I remember Mom and me living with Kookum after we left the shelter. Kookum used to call me her Little Muskwa, which means *Bear* in Cree. I remember her beading a pair of moccasins and a vest just for me.

"Is Kookum still around?"

"No, my son. She went to be with the Ancestors five years ago."

I freeze and stare straight ahead.

"She wanted to see you before she went and kept asking for you. But I didn't know where you were." She's quiet again for a moment. *"She gave me something to give to you if I ever see you again."*

"What is it?"

"It's a letter she's written to you. I want you to have it before I go back to Edmonton."

"When d'ya go back?"

"Next week."

My hands start to shake, and I'm feeling a pain and emptiness I haven't felt in a long time. I cry.

"Where are ya stayin', Mom?" I sniffle through tears.

"With my cousin, Phoebe in East Vancouver. Do you remember her?"

"Yeah. When did she move out here?"

"Two years ago," she says. *"Can I see you soon?"*

"Sure, Mom. Is tomorrow okay?"

"Yes. We'll see you tomorrow then, Warren. I am so happy. Phoebe's place is a co-op near the corner of Victoria Drive and East Pender Street. Her name is on the buzzer at the front."

"I'll see you and Phoebe tomorrow, Mom. I have uh well, I have an appointment, but I'll come to see you in the afternoon."

"We'll be here."

We say our goodbyes, and I slowly hang up the phone. I stare out to the deck where a black squirrel runs across the top of the rail of the patio, sits up on its hind legs and eats something. It stops, looks at me, and scampers off the rail to a nearby tree. My whole body is shaking. I feel a pressure building in my head. FUCK, tears are streaming from my eyes. Kookum is gone.

But it's like that little squirrel is Kookum, and she's telling me that life goes on. I feel lonely. I walk into the living room. I can hardly see through my tears as I flop onto the couch. I stare up to the ceiling and slump to one side on a cushion. Ozzy comes into the living room and jumps up on the couch beside me. He pokes at me with his paw like he's saying *hey, you okay, buddy?*

"You're a good buddy to me, Ozzy," I say to him, "you always know when I'm feelin' like shit, and you're here for me."

He curls up beside me and purrs. I cry.

20

I'm numb. I look around the waiting room of the doctor's office like it's the first time I've ever been in one. Dr. Chu said he wanted to see me right away. If there is a God out there, then I hope He's around me right now because my test results are in.

Then Dr. Chu appears. "Warren?" He is half-smiling, but with a sad look in his eyes. "Come in."

I walk into his office, and he gets me to sit in a chair in the corner while he closes the door.

"The results of your HIV test are back Warren…" He hesitates. "And I am sorry, but they're positive."

I feel my body sink.

"No, no fuckin' way! There's a mistake, that's wrong."

"As I've said before, there are such things as false positives, Warren. So, let's do another test just to be sure."

"Yeah, let's," I say. "This is wrong. I know it is."

"And it could very well be wrong, Warren," he says as he prepares another syringe. "But you need to be prepared just in case it isn't."

"What the fuck am I gonna do, Doc?" I'm terrified, and he can see it in my eyes.

"Let's wait till the results of the second test are in," he says. "That way, *if* it is false, you don't have to worry."

21

I walk through East Van with my headphones on. Icehouse's "Electric Blue" is playing from my Walkman, but the music is just background noise because my head ain't here. My test results keep swirling in my mind. This, changes everything in my life. I'm scared, and the questions keep coming at me.

What do I tell Daryl? What's he going to think of me now? Will he still love me? Is he even going to like me anymore? Is he going to kick me out? Am I going to be homeless?

What do I tell Mom? Is she going to want to know me anymore?

Are they even going to want to be around me anymore?

Am I going to lose my job because I work in a kitchen and the danger of cutting myself? FUCK!

Questions, and no answers. Dr. Chu says I shouldn't worry until the result of the second test are in, but I can't help it. Three more weeks of waiting! FUCK! If the tests come back positive again, that means I'll be dead in two years… and I haven't even started to live!

I'm walking, no, more like drifting through the part of town known as the Urban Rez because a lot of Natives live here. It's the area surrounding the corner of Commercial Drive and Venables Street. It's walking distance to the Vancouver Native Friendship Centre. I always liked this part of town, ain't no bullshit or pretenders like in Kerrisdale or Kitsilano.

Then before I know it, I arrive at the address Mom gave me. It's one of heaps of co-op housing units in this area, and this one is a

Native co-op. A wooden totem pole stands to the side of the front walk to the entrance as I approach.

I punch the number at the front security panel.

"Warren, is that you?"

"Yeah."

I'm buzzed through, and soon I knock on the door where Mom is staying. It flies open, and there she is with a big grin on her face. Just like I remember her. A small woman with long, greying hair. She's wearing a pair of jeans with a flowered blouse.

"Warren…" She is smiling and tears are streaming down her face.

We give each big a hug, then she kisses me on the cheek. I hold her tightly. My heart feels like it's ready to explode.

After all these years, finally, my mom!

She gently breaks our embrace. "You remember my cousin Phoebe?"

Phoebe takes the cigarette from her mouth and puts it in an ashtray. She comes over to the door and gives me a big bear hug. Phoebe's a bigger woman with a full head of beautiful black, curly hair and the odd streak of grey. She's wearing big, square 1970s style glasses. Somehow, they suit her.

"I'm so glad you came, Warren," Mom says.

I smile and take my headphones off.

"C'mon in," says Phoebe. "We got hot tea, and your mom made some chocolate chip bannock."

"Really? Chocolate chip bannock? Like Kookum used to make?" I say feeling a big smile on my face.

The smell of mom's fresh baking fills this place, and it feels like love. I have a quick look around the living room. In the corner, I see an easy chair with pieces of neatly folded leather and beading material.

I recognize some of the things hanging on the wall from when I was a little boy. There's a giant dream catcher that looks just like one that Kookum made, and it hangs in the living room window. There's a large, beaded pipe bag that hangs beside the door, and beside that, I recognize a wooden mask with wide eyes and cheeks puffed like it's blowing. I remember Kookum telling me that it was "to blow away any evil spirits that try to come through the door."

"Look at you," Mom says. "You've become such a handsome young man. Sit down."

"Do you take sugar in your tea?" Phoebe asks.

"Yeah, thanks." I say while I sit on the couch.

For so many years I've wanted so much to see my mom and Kookum again. And now we're here in the same room at the same time.

"How have you been?" Mom asks putting her hands over mine.

I look at the floor.

"Mom," I say, "my life ain't been so good."

I look at her as she puts her hand on my shoulder and gives me an understanding, loving smile.

"The government put me with Jenny and her awful family. I hated it there. I ran away and I lived on the street for a few years. I ended up in jail a couple times, Mom… I feel ashamed."

She sits closer to me and puts her arms around me.

"I have always loved you, and I always will love you, no matter what."

I feel like a little boy again. That little boy I lost somewhere back there, back when life was Mom, Kookum, and me. That little boy the government people hurt and shamed without end. That little boy the government people put in with Jenny, Pastor Ormand, and that psycho bunch.

The happy look on her face turns serious. "It has been many years, my son. There's something I really need to tell you."

"There's something I need to tell you too," I say.

"Warren, please let your mom speak." Phoebe is standing in the kitchen doorway. "It's important that you hear her."

She looks sadly at the floor then back to me. "I need to tell you that I love you and that I want you back in my life so much. I've missed you and always wondered what happened to you. Sometimes, I thought that I wouldn't see or hear from you again."

There's deep sadness on her face. "I've been sick," she says.

"What do you mean?" I ask.

She tries to tell me, but I can see it's hard for her to say anything.

Then Phoebe comes out of the kitchen and puts a small plate of chocolate chip bannock in front of me on the coffee table with a cup of tea. She sits to my other side on the couch, puts her arm around me and says,

"Warren, you should know that your mom has just found out she has cancer."

I glance up at Phoebe then over to Mom. Those words freeze me. I can't say nothing.

"The doctors have told me that I only have a couple of years left to live."

I stare straight ahead for a moment, look at the floor, then to Mom. I keep looking back and forth from the floor then to Mom. I don't know what to say. I don't know what to do. Just when we've found each other, she's going to leave me again.

"Please, Warren," Mom says, "please let me be a mom to you again. I tried, I really tried to look after you when you were growing up. I tried to have some money to put food on the table for you I tried to put nice clothes on you. I tried to protect you from your father but—"

"That drunken bastard!" I growl.

"Did you know your father told the government people that your mother was unfit to raise you?" Phoebe says. "That's why they got you when you were at school."

"Yeah, Mom said the bastard did that." I say. "And after him beatin' on Mom and me! I'll never forgive him."

"I never gave up on you."

"I know that now, Mom," I say feeling choked up again.

We hug each other tightly.

"Mom, I have something to tell you too. I, well, I've just been told I might have AIDS."

Mom's eyes are watering, and she weeps. Phoebe sits to one side of me, and Mom puts her arms around me and the three of us cry.

"I love you no matter what, Warren," she says through her tears.

Phoebe takes her glasses off, and wipes at them. "Why don't you give him that letter from his kookum."

Mom breaks our embrace, wipes her tears, smiles, and goes into the bedroom.

Quiet.

Mom comes back with an envelope and hands it to me. *To My Muskwa*, it says on the envelope. I open it. A small black and white photo slides out from the folded letter. I remember when this was taken. It's of Kookum and me when I was little, at one of those old photo booths at a shopping plaza in Edmonton. The sight of the two of us smiling at the camera makes me sad. I unfold the letter and read:

> Where is my Little Muskwa?
>
> My heart aches because I have not seen you for so long. I hope that, wherever you are, you are doing well, and life is treating you good. If this letter ever finds its way to you, I may be with the ancestors. But I want you to know that I have always loved you and I will always be there looking out for you as you walk on your journey. I don't have much to give you except my words, but they are given to you with love.
>
> Be careful in life, Warren. Don't walk the black road of alcohol and drugs because they will only break your spirit and lead to anger and sadness. Be kind to others because they will be kind to you. Be a good man even if others treat you bad and be true to your Creator because the Great Spirit will always be there. Please, always look after yourself and be good to your mother because you never know when you'll need her. Be strong in your heart, like the Muskwa I know you are.
>
> I'm sending you this picture to remind you that, whatever you go through in life, there are always happy times and there is always love. Whenever you doubt that, please look at this picture again to remind yourself of this. Love will always be there, even if you don't think it will be. The Creator did not

mean for us to suffer. To suffer means that we have forgotten who we are, and you always have choices in life. Be a strong man and be a good man, make the right choices.

Always remember, it doesn't matter what others might think of you, it's what you think about yourself that really matters. Be brave. Listen to your heart because that is the Creator speaking to you and hold on to your visions because they are what the Creator wants for you.

How I wish I could say these things to you in person, but you are not around, and I don't have much longer on this Earth. I will always love you my Little Muskwa, and I will always be with you.

With Love,

Your Kookum.

I shake once again, let go of the letter, and it drops on the floor. I rest my forehead in my hand. Before I know it, I'm crying again. I can feel Phoebe rubbing my back, and I can feel Mom put her arms around me again.

22

The morning sun streams into the bedroom, and even though it feels nice, I'm tired because I haven't slept all night. More like, I've been worried about everything all night. I look over to Daryl, and he's lying awake looking at the ceiling.

I went to see Dr. Chu yesterday afternoon because the results of my second HIV test arrived. I'm HIV Positive. In the meantime, Daryl's had two tests and they both came back negative. I guess because me and him have been using condoms. We had a good cry yesterday, and I still feel like crying. I turn and look at him again.

"What are you thinking about?" I ask.

"You know."

We're silent.

"I guess that means I only have a couple of years left," I mumble.

"I don't want to talk about it," he mumbles back.

I look at him beside me. "We have to."

He's silent.

I touch him.

"I'm afraid," I say. "I'm afraid this is gonna change everything between us."

He doesn't say anything and gives me a sad look. I feel a big lump in my throat.

"I'm… I'm afraid you're not, well… not gonna stick around," I say. "I'm afraid you're gonna leave me, and I'll get really sick and die alone."

He puts his arm around me. "You know, I love you. I haven't felt this way about someone for a long time… and now…"

"… I love you too," I say as I put my arm around him and we hold each other silently, closely, lovingly. Then after a long silence of holding each other, he sighs as he turns and looks at the ceiling again.

I start crying as he turns back to me.

"I've gotten to know you so well in what seems like a short amount of time," he says. "I've liked you since that night we met at the Castle. I've grown to love you. I love you being beside me. I love how you've always been, just you. I've always admired your fearlessness. The way you've always bounced back after major let-downs."

"But I'm a loser," I say.

"If you were a loser there's no way I'd be lying here with you right now. And there's no way I'm going to leave you. In spite of everything you may have done, or the things you've thought you've done, I look at you and see a wonderful guy who deserves to be loved."

My voice cracks. "I don't wanna go."

"I don't want you to go," he answers, his voice breaking.

We hold each other again like we'll never let go.

23

I know I ain't been no angel. Fuck knows I've been with a lot of guys since I've been out of the Slam! I've had a lot of sex with a lot of guys in the last couple of years. So, it's been tough for me to try to get hold of the guys whose names I can remember to let them know about what's happened with me. Yeah, and I've been called all kinds of shit as a result, like whore, slut, asshole, and even murderer in one case, when I *do* let people know!

Some have approached me to tell me that they have already… shit, what's the term, seroconverted! That doesn't stop them from giving me a severe blast of shit! I guess they're looking for anyone to put their blame and shame on, and I guess they figure I'm the guy. It's funny that this whole AIDS shit has brought out all the self-hating faggots who want to crucify their own kind. Insane!

But I ain't got time for any of that self-hating crap right now. This morning, for some reason, I've been thinking about Gil and Neil.

How do you find a person in a city as big as Toronto? How do you find that needle in the haystack? Where do you even begin? These are questions that cloud my head as I sit on the verandah bundled in a couple of sweaters and my denim jacket as the fall touches its cool, wet fingers to this city.

I feel cold, and even though I should go inside, something else is telling me to relax. My Walkman is playing George Harrison's "Got My Mind Set on You" while the cord of my headphones dangle around my neck.

I am feeling the need to get hold of Gil and Neil to tell them about what's happened to me. Since the three of us had sex together quite a few times, they need to know they should get tested. But what do I say to them if I get hold of them? *Hey Gil, I'm HIV and you might be too! Hey Neil, just thought I'd phone out of the blue and tell you I'm HIV now! Hey guys, how's it going? I'm HIV! You should get tested! Happy Thanksgiving!*

Are they even going to want to talk to me?

Just then the front door of the house opens and Hunter steps out carrying two mugs and hands one to me.

"Here's some hot chocolate, dear man," he says. "What are you doing out here in the cold?"

"Oh, hey, thanks Hunter." I take the mug and pull off my headphones. "I'm just thinkin' about how I'm gonna get hold of Gil and Neil in Toronto, and wondering how I'm gonna tell them about me, and to tell them to get tested."

Hunter sits on the porch with me and lights a joint he's taken from his pocket. He has a toke and passes it to me.

"Do you want a toke?"

"Sure, thanks," I say taking the joint from him.

"So, talk to me, dear man," he says. "Anything I can help with?"

I exhale. "I sure could use some advice about how to get hold of them. I don't even know where they are. I'm thinkin' they're in Toronto, but I don't know for sure."

"What makes you think they're in Toronto?"

"That's where Neil was living when we met him. I'm thinking they went back there."

"Well, remember your mom didn't know where you were, but she didn't give up for years until she finally found you. So, it is possible to find what you're looking for."

"I hope it's not gonna to take years because I don't have that long."

"Tell me about them," says Hunter.

"Gil and Neil?"

Hunter nods.

"What's to tell?"

“You obviously think highly enough of them, or you wouldn’t be sitting out here in the cold wondering how you’re going to contact them.”

I think about that for a moment.

“Yeah, I do think the world of both of those guys, man. And I’m so sorry that I let them down.”

“How did you let them down?”

“By ending up back in jail and maybe getting them in to trouble too.”

‘Well, tell me how you guys met.”

“I met Gil when I was in the slam the first time.”

“Did you know he was gay?”

“Not at first. I thought he was super good looking when we first met. Then him and me became really good buddies. For eighteen months, we had each-others backs while we were inside, and we became sex buddies too.”

“That was in Alberta?”

“Yeah. We both got released back to Calgary when we got out.”

“How does Neil fit into this picture?”

“We met him at a steam bath the day after me and Gil had our first meeting outside of jail.”

“A steam bath?”

“Yeah, me and Gil met up when I got out, went partying, and ended up there. Neil happened to be there too. He was visiting Calgary while on his way to Vancouver for a vacation.”

“Did the three of you have sex?”

“Not at first, well, we did the next day when we went for a drive in the Rockies to show Neil around. Then after that, yeah, quite a bit.”

“Unprotected?”

“Yeah, I mean we heard about this HIV stuff, but it was still somethin’ that didn’t really affect any of guys we knew back then. That was somethin’ in New York or San Francisco, not here.”

“How did you guys end up out here?”

"Neil asked us to go with him on his trip. Gil was out of the slam four months before me and wasn't havin' any luck finding work in Calgary."

"And what about you?"

"I didn't have nothin' special planned, and I was in the mood to party. After being in the slam for a couple of years, Neil's invite to join him in Vancouver was a ticket to party town for me."

Hunter sips his hot chocolate. "You guys got out here, then what?"

"We had fun! Man, did we have fun! It was my first time to Vancouver, and I wanted to sample everything I could."

"But you ended up in jail again. How did that happen?"

"I met these two guys at a bar one night and we got talkin'. Then next thing I know, I'm joining them down on Wreck Beach to sell dope. I'd done it before, and it was easy money. What I didn't know was the cops were watching those two for a while. This one morning they were waitin' for us when we left the beach."

I take a swig from my mug.

"They stopped us and told us to empty out knapsacks. I guess I panicked and started running. They caught me, arrested me, I told them to fuck off, and back inside I went for possession for purposes of trafficking and resistin' arrest."

Hunter looks like he's thinking about some things.

"Then Gil and Neil left you?"

"Yeah. I heard that Gil tried to see me when I was in Vancouver Remand, but a couple of the Screws gave him a hard time, and he dropped my shit off and then him and Neil left."

Hunter looks like he's in deep thought for a moment. Then he smiles.

"Maybe I can help you after all," he says.

"What do you mean?"

"I have a cousin who lives in Toronto, and he's gay…"

"Yeah?"

"He lives in the Gay Ghetto downtown, and he's really involved with all kinds of community stuff there."

"Yeah?"

"He knows a lot of people. So, do you mind if I ask him to have a scout-around to see if he might find them?"

"Fuck, no! That would be great!"

"You'll have to give me their full names and anything that you know about them that might help him while he's looking."

I move over and kiss him. "Thanks so much, Hunter. This would be great if it happens."

He giggles. "Well, thank me if and when he finds them."

24

It's been a couple of months since I was diagnosed, and it ain't been easy. I told Enzo at work that I was HIV-positive, and he got concerned that I would cut myself and contaminate the kitchen. Then he started in with shit like, "if you pray to God and promise Him you won't be gay anymore, maybe He'll forgive you."

That fucking hurt. I thought we had a better understanding than that. Then him and me had a fight, and I ended up quitting. I grew to love Enzo and his family. But I couldn't work there anymore. I came home and cried the day I left that place.

I don't have the regular paycheque I used to, and so the disability money I get from the provincial government every month is spent on shit like rent and bills. If I need extra stuff, I pretty much depend on the shit that landed me in the slam in the first place. I have that little grow op in the basement, nothing big, just enough to look after the few, trusted customers I do have. Cash only! The bastards in Ottawa already got enough from the money I did get! That's the way I roll, *and* it keeps food in the fridge!

I'm still working on that book, and it's going slower than I thought it would. But this morning's been great! I started writing and the words just kept coming!

> It was late one winter afternoon during one of our Saturday afternoon trips to the Royal to meet up with some of the other volunteers from the British Columbia Persons With AIDS Society. I've been volunteering there for a while and so were Ma and Phoebe. Daryl and Hunter were having their

usual draft beer and Ma, Phoebe, and me were having our coffee, tea, and pop. I overheard a couple of the guys talking with Phoebe about the beaded medallion one of the guys at the table had around his neck. It was of the Four Directions, four quarters of the circle coloured: Red, Yellow Black and White.

Phoebe said that she liked it and asked him where he got it from. He said that back in his hometown in Eastern Saskatchewan, he had a good friend whose family were First Nations. He got to know the family quite well and would often visit them.

One summer day they invited him over to their place to help put up their tipi. He was telling Phoebe that his friend's grandfather gave it to him for helping out that day. He always thought it was cool looking, but he never knew the story behind what it meant. He knew it had something to do with the four directions, but that was all he knew.

I remember Phoebe smiling and then telling him that was true—it did represent the four directions, and it also represented the Medicine Wheel. She explained that the Medicine Wheel represented a huge part of their spiritual teachings as Cree People. She said her kookum had taught her that the Cree People were given the teachings of the Medicine Wheel by the Creator.

The young fellow asked her if she knew what the Medicine Wheel meant.

She told him it meant being balanced.

"There are four parts of being human," she said. "They are the spiritual, physical, emotional, and mental, and it was important to have all these parts in balance to be complete as people."

She said that the centre of the Medicine Wheel represents your life's journey. And as she spoke, she kept pointing at the guy's medallion. She told him the Elders taught that the Medicine Wheel was life. "If you look at the Medicine Wheel, you start from yourself, and you look outwards and make your circle."

I remember by this time Daryl and a few others started listening to Phoebe speak.

"The Medicine Wheel," she said, "tells the story of how all life came to be. It rises like the morning sun in the east, following to the afternoon in the south, then moves to the evening in the west, and finally to the nighttime in the north. Then she pointed at the necklace once more. She explained the four colours on his medallion represented the four directions, the times of day, and the colours of the seasons: red for the spring and the east, yellow for the summer and the south, black for the fall and the west and white for the winter and the north."

I remember thinking that was the first time I heard her speak in this way.

She told us the four colours also represented the Creator's Children of the Earth: Red, Yellow, Black, and White. "The circle is not complete until everybody is in it..." this was her favourite saying and she said that it came from her teachings of the Medicine Wheel.

One of the guys at the table asked her why everything seemed so out of balance these days?

According to Phoebe "it was that way because too many people only look after two directions of themselves, the mental and physical. Many people forget to look after their spiritual side and because of that, they don't know how to deal with their emotions."

One of the guys asked if that was why there are so many angry people these days.

Phoebe smiled. "Our emotions speak the truth about who we really are, and because of that, they make us feel vulnerable, and anger hides that truth. Our real emotions are the part of us that feels truth about what is going on around us. So, we have learned to hide our true selves, and our emotions and replace them with anger because anger is easier to deal with."

I spoke up. "Didn't the elders take years to know everything there is to know about the Medicine Wheel, the Sundance, and the Sweat lodge?"

Phoebe was always cool and kept a smile on her face, and told me that's what people believe, but being spiritual is to remember where we came from and being thankful for the gifts given to us by the Creator. Remember that your first gift when you came in to being was your spirit. We get into trouble when we take our spirits for granted and neglect them."

Talk about wowing a group to the point of silence. The guy wearing the Medicine Wheel symbol clasped his hand over it. Phoebe smiled and told him to wear that grandfather's gift with humility and gratitude. She told the young man that the grandfather obviously saw something within him to give him such a beautiful and powerful symbol of spirituality.

She told that us she was taught a prayer that went with the four directions on the Medicine Wheel, and she recited it for us. When she was through, once again, the group was silent, and one of the guys asked her to write it down for us. One of the waiters had stopped what he was doing and was listening in on the conversation. When she had written the prayer down, he offered to take it in the back office and make copies for everyone. We all liked that idea. So, he took it and brought photocopies back for us all.

"Great Spirit, teach us to be like the four directions. Teach us to be like the east where the sun rises every day, reminding us to bring light to the world. Teach us to be like the south where the sun is warm, reminding us to be warm and kind to one another. Teach us to be like the west where the sun sets every day, to remind us to rest that we may gather strength for ourselves and others. And teach us to be like the north where the cool winds blow that reminds us to be refreshing to all those we meet. All My Relations."

25

Daryl figured that if I'm going to be writing a book, I should be going to bookstores and scouting around for shit to read. But I'll be fucked if I knew what I wanted to read. So naturally, I started with Little Sister's the gay bookstore here in Vancouver, and started talking to Jim Deva, one of the guys who owns the place. I told him I was writing this book, and him and me talked about what it was about.

He showed me some of the books they had in stock, and a little about bestselling gay authors, like Armistead Maupin, Jane Rule, Larry Kramer, John Rechy, Brad Gooch, and a shitload of others. He told me stories about some of the authors, and then we talked more about my book.

He told me about several events that happen around the city every month. They're like café nights where people drink coffee, eat sweets, and listen to some local musicians, poets, and writers, while they read the shit they wrote. Sort of like the old beatniks used to do. Anyways, he tells me to come out the next time and read something I've been working on.

I told him that I'd think about it.

I got talking with Daryl, and the way he saw it, the more I kind of acted like a writer, the better chance I would have of publishing something. That was a weird concept for me, and I didn't understand it at first. But the more I thought about that idea, the more I liked it. But fuck, getting up in front of a whole lot of strangers and reading my shit? That was like, I don't know, getting naked in front of everyone.

I remember that first reading. There I was, sitting in the audience and watching the crowd come in. Fuck, they just kept coming.

Me…

Reading…

In front of all these people…

And the crowd is growing!

Where the fuck was my head?

That must have been wicked shit I was smoking when I made up my mind to do this!

I thought, *Someone get me out of here…*

Anyways, I made it through the reading. A lot of the audience liked what they heard, and some of them just sat there looking like they never heard any of this kind of shit before. So, since then, I've done a couple more. I'm starting to like reading shit in front of people. And I like talkin' to everyone after. It's good to hear that people are liking the shit I'm writing. But folks are always asking me when the book will be published, and I ain't sure what to tell them, so I say I'm hoping to have it out soon.

Meanwhile, with my pot sales, I made enough money to make a couple of trips up to Edmonton to see Mom. It was weird being back in the old town. So many memories, most of them bad. I was always glad to be on the bus back to Vancouver after only a couple of days. I sure miss Mom though. Daryl and Mom have had a few chinwags on the phone, and we've had Phoebe over for dinner a few times so we could all get to know each other better.

The last time she was over, she had a big, honking smile on her face the whole time. Like she knew something I didn't.

So, I asked her what was up with that smile. "Next time you talk to your mom," she said, "ask her about the other thing your kookum left for you?"

"What is it?" I asked.

"Oh, wait and see," she answered with that knowing smile.

So, when I next spoke with Mom and I asked her and she said, "wait till the next time you come up here, and I'll show you. I want it to be a surprize!"

So, the last time I went to Edmonton, Mom gave me the beaded, moose hide jacket that Kookum made for Mooshum (my grandfather). Mom said the time was right for me to have it. I remembered it from when I was a little kid. The moose hide was like gold as the sun shone on it. It was covered back and front with Kookum's beadwork, and leather fringes ran along the bottoms of the sleeves, and across the front and back of the jacket. I tried it on, and even though it was too big (Mooshum was a big man), it felt like home. It felt like love. I love that jacket and started wearing it lots.

Over the last couple of weeks, Daryl and me been talking about the possibility of Mom living closer to us. Seemed like a good plan for her to move down here from Edmonton so we can be closer, good for her and good for me.

After me and Daryl had our last talk about it, I phoned Mom in Edmonton to tell her. She got all excited and said she'd see if Phoebe and her could live together.

Next thing Daryl and me knew, Phoebe was phoning us all excited. She loved the idea and put in a request to get a two-bedroom apartment at her co-op for her and Mom. Since it could be a while before they get the bigger place, her and Mom were going to share Phoebe's one bedroom place.

And now here we are—me, Phoebe, and Daryl, waiting in line here at the bus terminal. I'm going up to Edmonton for a week to help Mom get ready for the move down here. I talked to her on the phone last night, and we're both real excited. She's been packing her stuff and getting ready for this for a few weeks now. The movers will be at her place in a couple of days and are going to drop her stuff at our place. We'll store it in the basement, and she can take what she needs, when she needs it.

Dr. Chu's agreed to be our doctor, and so we got all her medical records transferred to Vancouver through his office.

We're waiting in front of the sleeping bus for my twenty-hour ride to Edmonton, when Daryl bumps shoulders with me. "You know, I'm really excited about this."

"Same here," I say, "best thing in the world to do."

Phoebe smiles and says, "This *is* the best thing to happen. Who better to understand what you're feelin', when your mom's goin' through the same thing? Who better to know where you've come from and understand the way you are than the woman who took you from house to house to a shelter to escape your father?"

I smile at Phoebe and give her a big hug.

The bus driver goes on to the Greyhound and turns the ignition. The bus roars to life as the driver gets back out while the vehicle idles. I'm about fifth in line, and there's maybe ten people behind me.

"I guess you'll be boarding soon," Daryl says.

"Yep, I've been thinkin' about how things will be different once Mom moves to Vancouver."

"It'll be like a family with all of us together," says Phoebe.

"Okay folks," the bus driver yells, "have your tickets ready and put the luggage that is to go underneath the bus just to the side over here." He points to an area where two guys wait to load suitcases.

"I'd hug ya," I say to Daryl, "but we'd get the shit kicked out of us."

"When has that ever stopped you?" he smiles.

I laugh and we hug.

"Don't forget to feed Ozzy," I say.

He nods.

I look at Phoebe. "You make sure he keeps out of trouble while I'm gone."

She laughs. "Don't worry, Daryl and I have a lot to do in this next week. So, he'll be too busy."

Daryl smiles and nods in agreement. "Don't worry," he says, "a week goes by fast anyway."

I smile and nod as the line starts moving forward. The driver takes my ticket and puts an *Edmonton* tag on my luggage. I put my suitcase beside the bus where one of the waiting guys then sticks it underneath the vehicle. I get on board and find a window seat to park myself.

Once everyone's on, the driver gets on the bus, shuts the door, and hits the horn twice as he backs out of the parking stall. I wave to Daryl and Phoebe, and they wave back to me. We pull out of the parking lot and turn on to Terminal Avenue, then drive east out of the city.

I put on my headphones, stick a tape in my Walkman and turn it on. George Michael sings "Kissing a Fool." I'm feeling pretty happy. It feels good to have Mom and Phoebe back in my life again. I feel loved. I feel like I'm wanted.

As we travel eastward out of the city, we pass a sign with Rupert Park painted on it. Fuck, I remember seeing that sign when Gil, Neil, and me arrived in Vancouver back in 1983! Man, have times ever changed, and they're changing again. My life has been a long and crazy road, but here I am, and here I go to a new life with Mom, Phoebe, Daryl, Hunter, and Ozzy.

I take a deep breath and lean on to the window. Shutting my eyes, I smile and let George sing to me.

PART SIX

Daryl Kellerman – March 2005

March, and it looks like cold day to boot. Well, at least it's not raining.

I gaze at the outside world from my living room window, sip my morning coffee, and look over to the apartment buildings that line the shore of English Bay a couple of blocks away. I can just see the top few floors of each of them as the West End of Vancouver is undergoing drastic change these days. It seems that every available city lot now has a condo tower standing on it. All the cozy little low rise apartment buildings have now been relegated to the annals of history.

I've been thinking about Warren since I woke up this morning.

You know, had I not gone to the Castle Pub that night way back when, I never would have met him. Truth is, I didn't really want to go out for happy hour that evening. It was one of those *oh-what-do-I-have-to-lose* moments. And I don't regret any of it.

Life with Warren was an adventure, and through all that, I watched him grow. It was almost like watching a boy grow into adulthood before my eyes. But in retrospect, I shouldn't have been surprised. He was ten years younger than me. There was still a lot of that juvenile smart-ass attitude there, and his occasional hot-headed temper tantrums could be hard to take. But he knew he wanted something better in life than what he had, something real that he could believe in. I think that was when he really started getting serious about publishing his journals into a book.

As he was writing them, he was trying, mostly unsuccessfully, to organize them so he could eventually get help putting everything together for his book. Organization was never one of his strong points. When Ma and Phoebe appeared on the scene, that added a deeper dimension to his life that he had never felt before. The three of them getting to know each other all over again meant he was getting to know who he really was, and that made him happy, probably for the first time in his life!

What can I say about Ma and Phoebe? Ma's focused determination in finding her only child, even decades after he was taken by Social Services was awe-inspiring, and the fact that Phoebe helped her, believed in her, and supported her for all those years, well, I am still in awe of the two of them.

I finish what remains of my coffee in one gulp and think about this coming evening because tonight, for the first time, I'm going to be reading Warren's book in public! I'm nervous as hell about it, but here it is, finally a reality after all these years. What a journey it has been to get it published! It's like publishers in general didn't want to hear from anyone who was queer, Métis, and an ex-con… until one of them finally did! And even when I got the initial notice from them, I didn't believe it. When I think of what it took to bring Warren's various scattered and mostly unorganized journals to a solid book, I'm amazed I was successful at achieving it in the first place.

This reading is going to be at the Main Branch of the Vancouver Public Library downtown, and I'm still not sure which portion of the book that I will be reading tonight. There are going to be several authors reading their works tonight in celebration of an event called *Authors Unbound, New Writers in Vancouver!* It's fitting that this event should be held tonight because this is the fourteenth anniversary of Warren's passing… and it seems like only yesterday that it happened. Where has the time gone?

Anyway, it's time for my daily walk. I go to the hall closet in my small West End apartment; today I'm wearing the moose hide jacket that Warren's kookum made for his grandfather. Ma gave it to me after Warren's Celebration of Life. I was honoured and humbled to receive it, and I wear it only during special occasions like today. Every year at this time, I celebrate who he was, and I celebrate his mom and the love she showed him. Not only for being a mom to him again but being one of his best friends ever.

I'll always be grateful to Ma and Phoebe for being so close to him and caring for him during the last couple of years of his life, even though Ma needed just as much attention. Ma and Warren were both so happy when they found each other. It was like a huge hole they had carried in their hearts for years was finally mended.

So many things have changed in this city since that time. Luckily, I've had several of Warren's dog-eared journals sitting on the coffee table, not to mention his book, which helps me remember some of the details of our lives together. There are times, before the book was published, that I would take one of those journals out, just like Warren did during his last couple of years of life, and randomly read it. They were all about his life, like this portion:

> I was a little boy hiding in the bushes behind the school. I must have been, maybe, seven or eight years old. I was being hunted by two social workers along with a couple of cops—and I was afraid. They found me and took me from my hiding place. I was crying and screaming, "Let go of me! Put me down! Fuckin' let go of me! HELLLLP!"
>
> I got taken from Mom and Kookum. No one ever told me why. Whenever I asked, I'd get told, "None of your business!"

I let all that sink in. This is shit that I never had to contend with when I was that age.

I've got my memories, and admittedly, many are getting fuzzy as I grow older. Try as I might, I have some difficulty remembering details from those years with Warren. Lots of things are now a blur. So, in reading these journals, I've remembered a lot of details.

I cried hard when he passed, even though his passing was expected. Why is it when someone you care for dies, you can feel just how expansive the Universe really is? What is it about the death of a loved one that makes you feel eternity all around you? It's almost like an alone-in-the-Universe feeling when everything about your life has just been turned upside down and then it explodes. You have no idea what lies ahead of you, so you focus on the here and now, and that's where the expansive feeling comes from. Focussing on the here-and-now was what got me through the worst of the grief after he died.

But then I could hear Warren's voice saying, *"Quit feelin' sad. I'm okay, get over it. Take care of Ma and Phoebe..."* just as if he were standing beside me.

As I remember those times, I feel sad for a time that is no more. The parties, the house we lived in, the events we attended, the people who are no longer around—I miss them the most. Back then, I hated that AIDS shit had been destroying my community, especially during those years in the late 1980s and early 1990s! That's when all kinds of people I knew were dying from it, everywhere I turned, it seemed. I'm lucky. I emerged from that time unscathed, in that all these years later I'm still HIV negative. When Warren and I were together, we did practice safe sex, and I believe that's what's kept me from becoming positive.

I hated the religious leaders who talked about Christian love and acceptance, but had no compassion in their hearts, except for those who had the money to buy their way into church coffers!

I hated the politicians who marginalized us gays just to garner more votes so they could have a job for the next few years. And I hated the media when it ended all its news reports on AIDS as being *a disease that is found amongst gay and bisexual men...* every goddamn time they reported on it. It only fanned the flames of society's hostility towards us! But I guess that type of shit meant ratings, and *that* meant more money! I still carry a lot of hate around and don't trust any of those institutions because, when push came to shove, they showed their true colours toward us.

I stop to look in the mirror by the apartment door and stare at the blond-turning-white hair that I still have. It has been thinning on top of my head over the last handful of years, and I've noticed I have developed crow's feet to the outside of both of my eyes. Looking older, Daryl, looking older. But the crow's feet let people know that you smile a lot… at least that's what I like to tell myself as I go out to the hall.

The seagulls squawk and soar in circles around the immediate area, like they're singing to the day as I exit the apartment building. A guy zips by on a hoverboard dressed in full motorcycle gear with an old boom box strapped to his back with "Bring it Home" by Swollen Members blasting from it. I don't know where he's going, but he zips by every morning about this time. Warren would have liked that song, though. He got into Hip-Hop just before he passed. His favourite record was *It Takes a Nation of Millions to Hold Us Back* by Public Enemy.

"This shit's real," he'd say. "I can relate to what they're sayin'!" He especially liked "Don't Believe the Hype." To this day, I swear I still know all the songs off that album by heart because Warren played it so much.

I've long since moved out of that old place in East Van where the bunch of us spent many happy times together, and I now live in this small apartment here in the West End, only a couple of blocks from English Bay. In fact, that's where I first head to on these daily walks. I smirk as I notice people turning their heads as they look at the ornate jacket I wear. It always turns heads with its golden coloured moosehide, elaborate beadwork and fringes, and man is it heavy! It must weigh about thirty pounds! I find an empty bench overlooking the beach at English Bay and settle in comfortably as I just take in everything going on around me.

"Hey," says a young First Nations man as he passes by me, "nice jacket you got there."

"Thanks."

"I'll bet there's a story to that!"

"There is," I say, "it belonged to my late partner. His grandmother made it for his mooshum."

His eyes grow wide. "Oh man," he says excitedly, "was he Cree?"

"His mom was."

"Wow, is that moose hide?" he asks while excitedly touching it.

"It is."

"Must be a *real* story to this jacket then."

"You wanna hear it?" I ask.

He hesitates but only for a moment.

"Sure," he says and sits beside me.

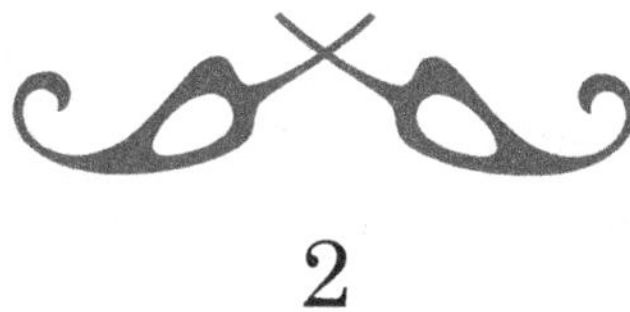

2

The young guy stuck around for a little bit, then yawned, bid me goodbye, and moved on thanking me. As he was about to leave, he asked me if I had a smoke I could give him, and I gave him one of my joints instead. One would have thought that I just handed him a million dollars he was so thrilled. After he left, I sat alone, took another joint from my pocket, and sparked it while taking in the view of English Bay.

I eventually got up and made my way here, to Delaney's, a coffee shop where a lot of the local Queer folk gather. This has become part of my routine. I go in, find a lone stool by one of the front windows, sip my coffee, eat my muffin, and people watch for a while. The band Outkast sings "Hey Ya!" from the coffee shop speakers, and I think about a lot about Warren while I sit here.

I think about the day Warren arrived back from Edmonton with Ma. I thought they were both going to burst as we met them at the bus terminal. They said they had been laughing and joking on the bus all the way down from Edmonton. It was to the point where a couple of the other passengers asked them to tone it down, a couple of times.

They were so happy to be together as mom and son again. They became inseparable. It wasn't too long after Ma arrived in town, we all decided that every Thursday and Friday would be Ma's time over for a visit with us. It was to give Phoebe her weekly alone time. Ma would come over to our place for dinner and she would stay the night, then I would drive her back to Phoebe's after dinner on Saturday.

And Ma always insisted on sleeping on the hide-a-bed couch in the living room, even though we offered her our bed.

If there are such things as guardian angels, Ma and Phoebe turned out to be Warren's. I remember Phoebe became an auntie to Warren, Hunter, and me. We became a family, looking out for each other, and making sure we were always in good health and spirits. It was the five of us who initially pooled our resources to come up with enough money to hire movers to pack Ma's things and move her furniture down to Vancouver and our basement.

I'll never forget how excited everyone was, especially Warren and Ma. I got choked up several times the day they arrived from Edmonton, just watching them chatter, giggle and laugh out loud like two excited children. Phoebe said, "the circle is not complete until *everyone* is in it." And that's how it felt with the five of us.

After Phoebe and I picked them up from the bus depot that day, we went right over to Phoebe's place. She, Hunter, and I had worked all morning preparing a late celebratory lunch/early dinner for us.

The whole thing had been a heartwarming experience for me as I watched Warren and Ma get to know each other all over again. The afternoon was spent sharing memories of when Warren was a little boy. Memories of his kookum and his boyhood in Edmonton. There was laughter and some tears too. Especially when the subject of his father came up. That was still a deep wound for them—one that hadn't healed all those years later.

"All I can do is find it in my heart to forgive him," I remember Ma said choking on the emotion that was welling in her.

"I'll *never* forgive that bastard for what he done to us," Warren responded. "After beatin' on Ma and me, he gets pissed off and sics the government workers on us cuz he can't get to us in the shelter!"

"Your mom is right, Warren," Phoebe calmly said. "Try to find it in your heart to forgive. It's never good to carry anger around like that."

Warren sat in silence looking straight ahead with his eyebrows furrowed, like he was reluctantly thinking about it, but still didn't want to hear it.

Phoebe was always wise and had a delicious sense of humour. I remember laughing so hard when she would tell us about some of the antics her and Ma would get up to when they were much younger in back in Alberta.

"I remember when your ma and me were teenagers," she said to Warren, "we'd be getting ready to go to a local dance, but first, we'd have to put on our war paint."

"War paint?" Warren asked.

"Our makeup," Phoebe giggled.

"Remember what your mom always said to us?" Ma asked Phoebe.

She chuckled. "She used to tell us, 'Remember to be careful when you're out in the world. Always be yourself, and don't be like the White people. They shit in their houses and eat outside.'"

We all laughed.

For all the shit the three of them went through in their lives, their spirits were resilient. And I grew to love them all very much.

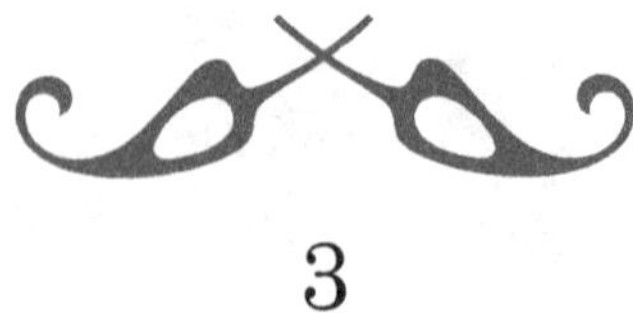

3

Meantime back to the present moment at Delaney's, "Rock Steady" by Remy Shand is now playing over the speakers, and I notice a copy of a the *Westender* in a small heap on the counter nearby. I drag it over in front of me, and immediately see an ad for a local bathhouse. I chuckle right away as I'm reminded of a conversation about the bathhouses that Warren and I once had. This one night when we were stoned, we got talking about bathhouses, and some of the experiences we've had during the various trips we took to the *sin bin*, as we liked to call it.

Warren recounted how he and Bert met Neil at a bathhouse in Calgary. And that's how he got out to Vancouver. I told him one of the weirdest incidents I had in a bathhouse was fucking this guy who wouldn't shut up the whole time.

Warren chuckled.

"The moment the guy was quiet," I said, "I'd just get into some serious pounding his ass, and he'd start talking again."

Warren chuckled again.

"You should have seen him. At one point, this guy grabbed a pack of cigarettes from his pants pocket, took one out and began smoking it. 'That feels good, by the way,' he says like he was commenting on the weather."

Warren laughed out loud.

I hadn't seen him laugh that hard before. "Don't tell me," Warren said, "then the guy takes out a couple of slices of bread from his shoulder bag and starts makin' a fuckin' sandwich!"

Now I laughed out loud and clapped my hands together, while Warren tried to continue, but was laughing so hard that he couldn't compose himself long enough.

"... then, he... then he... talks about the stock market while eating a sandwich while getting a dick in the ass at the tubs!"

We both laughed out loud.

"Then," I said, "he brings a ball of yarn and a pair of knitting needles out of the bag he had beside him..."

"... AND STARTS KNITTIN' A FUCKIN' SWEATER WHILE GETTIN' FUCKED!" Warren roared.

He collapsed to his side and lay on the couch laughing with tears streaming down his face.

I giggle as I think of that time. Man, that was in 1988! Again, where's the time gone?

The XV Winter Olympic Games were in Calgary that year. I remember Warren and I being glued to the TV whenever we could, to watch the various events. Then in the evenings, when I was out at gigs, Warren and Hunter would have Ma and Phoebe over watching the highlights of the day's events while munching on popcorn, chips and drinking pop. Ma and Phoebe would especially like to watch the men's figure skating event.

"Oh, they're so handsome," Ma would say.

"And they have nice bums," Phoebe would add while smiling. Ma would giggle in agreement.

Katarina Witt, from what was then East Germany, was one of the stars of those Olympic Games. She won the gold medal for figure skating, and her amazing costuming was the subject of interesting talk in the media. The costumes ranged from whimsical and flowing, to Victoria's Secret/black leather-like erotic. I remember watching her and thinking, *Man, if I were straight...*

The other stars of those Olympic Games that year were Eddie the Eagle from England, and the first appearance of the Jamaica Bobsleigh Team in an Olympic Games.

Eddie the Eagle was the first British Competitor in Ski Jumping since 1928. He placed last, and that record stuck to him for years. Meanwhile, there was a movie made, loosely based on the Jamaica Bobsleigh Team at the Calgary Winter Olympics called *Cool Running*. It starred John Candy and was one of his last roles before he died.

I flip the page of the paper and smile because there's an article here by a guy I've gotten to know in the last couple of years. About six months ago, Noel managed to get himself a weekly gig, and he calls himself *The Old Bastrich!* His character is a miserable, sarcastic old crank that, in the beginning, informed the public of what the most entertaining things to do around town were… whether we liked it or not and with all the finesse and sophistication, a miserable old coot can muster. What it has become is a bi-weekly rant from a crotchety, old curmudgeon. I start reading and almost immediately chuckle. I have to admit, he's quite entertaining, especially with today's rant against his favourite subject: Vancouverites and their weirdness.

> *I've always said Vancouver is the only city I know where the citizens constantly forget to take their meds!*

I further chuckle as I continue to read today's rant:

> … *And I do not understand the particularly bizarre habit that Vancouverites have, of standing under store awning with their umbrellas up over their heads! Why the hell do the boneheads keep doing this? Well, I assume it is so their umbrellas won't get wet while waiting for the bus! I think all the rain that this town gets, has mushed the brains of every person who lives in Vancouver.*

He's told me that he's already getting a lot of mail, most of it from people who think he's a hoot, and others… not so. He got an email from one lady who thought he should be fired then have his mouth washed out with soap. He had a good laugh over that one.

"Hey Papi," says a familiar voice. I look up from the paper to see Brady smiling at me.

"Brady! What are you doing here? I mean, how are ya?" I say standing up and hug him.

Brady and I have had a long-term, and I might add passionate, affair that was put on hold a couple of years back when he went off to art school in Toronto. I've thought about him a lot since he's been away, and we have kept in touch. He always said that he was coming back to Vancouver to live when his studies were over. I just didn't expect to see him so soon.

"I recognize that jacket," he says. "You're still wearing it to mark his passing?"

"Yep, today's the day."

"I remember some of the stories you told me about him."

"Well, I still miss him. Under all his bravado he was a great guy. Anyway, I'm so glad to see *you* again! What are you doing here? You back for a visit?"

"Nope, back in town for good!"

"What? You're done school?"

"Yep, done for good.

"Didn't work out the way you thought?"

"Y'know, I thought art school would be more creative, maybe even nurturing..."

"I remember you telling me. So, it wasn't all you hoped it would be?"

"It was more hard-assed and cutthroat than I was willing to put up with. I wasn't into that shit and, more to the point, didn't sign up for it. I realised that the art school shit doesn't work for me. So, I've quit and come back. Missed being Vancouver too much," he says with a smile. "Missed you too." Leaning in, he kisses my cheek.

Brady's a fellow musician, and we met at local music festival. The mutual attraction was immediate. When talking to him, I found out that, like me, he plays guitar and keyboards, loves the music of Django Reinhardt, Fred Hersch, and Len Aruliah. And he can't get enough of Jean-Luc Ponty, Herbie Hancock, Thelonius Monk, and Billie Holiday. He's thirty-three and has thick, unkempt, brown hair and a square jaw with constant five o'clock scruff. His wire-rimmed glasses only accentuate his big doe eyes, his athletic body is tight and lean, and he's a very sweet man. He's looking just as good now as he ever did! It feels good to be holding him again.

"I've missed you too… a lot."

All those old feelings, feelings that I'd put aside because I thought it would be years before I would ever see him again, are all flooding back.

"It's good to have you back, Brady."

"It's good to be back, Papi."

I've always liked it when he's called me that. I smile. "That's my boy. Why don't you join me?"

"I'd love to," he says as he pecks me on the cheek again, and we gently break our embrace and sit on the stools facing each other.

"So," I say, "how long *have* you been back?"

"Not long, a couple of days."

"But why didn't you let me know you were back in town?"

"I wanted to surprize you."

"You've done that alright. Where you staying?"

"Sleeping on my sister's couch for now."

"How is Shelagh doing?"

"She's doing great. Her and her boyfriend are getting along great. They're living together, so I don't wanna stay there too long. Their place is small, and I don't want to wear out my welcome."

"I hear ya."

I look at those brown eyes and crooked little smirk of his.

"Why don't you to stay with me until you get settled around."

"I was hoping you'd say that." His smirk blooms into a full smile.

"I know."

"Is right away too soon?"

"No, it's not too soon, you can bring your stuff over whenever you'd like to, my boy. So, what do you think you'll do now that you're back?"

He shrugs. "I don't know, Papi. I'm gonna lay low for a couple of days to figure things out. First thing I wanna check out is to see if

I can get my old job back at the courier company just to make some money in the meantime," he says. "So, you still got your keyboards?"

"Yep, I like to play at least three times a week. You?"

"My guitar is back at my sister's place. We can jam like we used to."

"I'd like that," I say. "But you know how those jam sessions always ended."

"Yep," he says, "with us in the sack."

I look at him, and I can't help but think how good-looking and sexy is and feels. He's always had this effect on me. I'm grateful that he likes being with me. We certainly click together. I put my hand on his knee. He smiles and puts his hand on top of mine.

"I thought a lot about you while I was away," he says. "So, when I quit school and came back here, all I wanted to do was see you again."

"And here I am."

"And here you are."

"Can I stay with you tonight, Papi?"

"I do have something going on tonight…"

"Oh," he says sounding disappointed.

"Actually, I'm reading at the library tonight. Why don't you come along and listen, then we can go back to my place?"

"What are you reading?"

"Remember I was putting together Warren's book?"

"Did you finish it?"

"Yep, it's published, and tonight is the first reading."

"COOL! Yeah, I'd like to come and listen. Can I buy a signed copy?"

"I'll give you one when we get back to my place."

"Wow, you're a musician, author, *and* a painter once upon a time too," he says. "How cool is that?"

"By the way," I ask indicating the service counter with my hand, "do you want a coffee or something to drink?"

He moves in closer to me smiles, runs his hand up my arm. "I'd rather be having you."

"You haven't changed a bit. That's why I've always liked you."

He lowers his voice. "Let's go back to your place where you can order me to take my clothes off."

My pulse quickens. He always did like playing the completely passive role and loves it when I get bossy with him. A broad smile draws across my face. "I've always liked the way you think."

4

We lay in bed talking about Warren's book. I've just finished reading a passage from it.

"That's an interesting title for the book," Brady says, "did Warren always want to call it that?"

"Yeah, he did."

"Why *Last Chance Town*?"

"It was something our roommate at the time suggested, and he liked it."

"Now that the book is published, are you going to keep his journals?"

"Yeah, there are a couple of them sitting to the side of the coffee table. The ones that have the green and black covers."

"I remember you were really into putting his journals together when you brought those two boxes of his out of storage."

"Yeah, and even though it took all that time to go through them, I managed to get them in some semblance of order to make a story of his life."

"It must have been tough for you to do that."

"It was, sometimes. A lot of his inner feelings went into those journals, so sometimes it was challenging to decide what I should put in the manuscript, and what to leave out… if anything. And sometimes it would get emotional for me, but luckily, not often. Of course, reading his chicken scratch was something else, and really taxing at times. I somehow managed to get through it, but too many times I couldn't make out words, or even full sentences."

"What did you do when that would happen?"

"I would try my best to decipher what he was trying to say. Admittedly, sometimes I had to guess at what he had written."

Then I look at Brady, his naked body snuggled into my side with my arm around him. I look at the tattoos that adorn a lot of his torso and arms.

I point at a tattoo of a merman. "That's new."

He looks at it. "Yeah, I got that done when I was still in Toronto. Nice one, eh?"

"Yeah, that's a really nice one."

He looks up at me and kisses me again.

"Could you read a little more from his book to me?"

I'm a bit taken back because I was expecting him to want some more action.

"Are you sure?" I ask.

"Yeah, I wanna hear some more."

I smile as I reach over to the side table, retrieve my reading glasses, open the book to a random page, because I think I know where this is going to go. I read to him once more.

> I've been complaining to Daryl and Ma lately that I've been feeling useless. I got no more job to go to everyday, and I'm having a tough time finding things to keep me occupied. I feel like I want to do more than just put together shit for my book.
>
> I've been kind of worried about my health and how much longer I'm going to stick around. Ma says I need something to centre me, make me more focussed.
>
> Daryl convinced me to see what kind of community support I could get, so I went to speak with Dr. Chu, who's been encouraging me to register with AIDS Vancouver. He figures that, by me doing this, I can be plugged into what resources could be available to me, and he told me he would support me with any kind of letters that need to be written, etc.

So, I went down to their office and had a long talk with one of the volunteers there. I went to a couple of their meetings, and it was at one of them that I picked up a newsletter put out by the British Columbia Persons with AIDS Society BCPWA as it was known then.

Anyways, I'm reading the mission statement: a grassroots group which encourages Persons with AIDS to empower themselves by advocating for their rights and their health. From our personal struggles and challenges come our courage and strength…

and I felt something.

I can't explain to you what it was, exactly, but I could almost feel flames burning in my belly. It felt like something in me got lit. I still can't explain it, but I like it.

"You know what?" I said at the dinner table that night.

"What?" asked Ma.

"I'm gonna volunteer at the BCPWA! I'm gonna help raise funds and help people out!"

"My son, the Warrior." Ma smiled.

"I mean it, Ma. I ain't gonna stand by and let people die for no reason!"

The next day me, Ma, and Phoebe went down to the BCPWA office so I could register as a volunteer.

While there, we got talking to a guy named Steve who gave us a tour of the office and facilities. Before we left, Steve gave me a volunteer form to fill out. I guess that Steve must have got Ma and Phoebe inspired because they filled out a form to volunteer too. I think that turned out to be one of the best things we could have all done. Because it made me feel like I was doing something, and we got to know a lot of the other volunteers, and we all became friends too.

My reading is interrupted by Brady pushing the book away and planting a deep kiss on me. I figured this would happen. Brady's probably the only person the world who gets turned on by people reading to him. I put the book aside and take him in my arms.

5

After we played, I dozed off and I had a dream about Warren. There he was, that crooked grin on his face, telling me in his own inimitable way…

"Man, I was at this bonus fuckin' sex party last night! There were all these hot fuckin' studs and they were horny as hell. You shoulda been there Kellerman! Ya woulda liked it!"

That's when I woke up and laughed! Warren once told me that if there was such a thing as Heaven, he hoped it would be a continuous hot, raunchy orgy with lots of hot studs. That was so Warren.

Then I look beside me to find that Brady is not there. I get out of bed and go into the living room to see him lying on the couch with my housecoat on, reading a copy of Warren's book. He quickly glances up at me. "I picked up reading from the part you read to me about where him, Ma, and Phoebe started doing volunteer work at the BCPWA."

"It always feels like he's in the same room talking to me whenever I read his book," I say.

When Brady doesn't respond, I sit beside him on the couch. "You know, I think that was about the time that I saw Warren start to become a star before my eyes."

"Become a star?" he asks.

"Yeah, he really started growing as a person. He really began to know who he really was. And that's star material in my world."

"It sounds like you guys had a great life together."

"It was," I say, "we had our toughs, but the five of us were happy."

"I would have liked to have met him."

"He would have liked you," I say. "He had a thing for guys he considered talented or intelligent. That really turned him on."

"It's not like I'm intelligent or anything," Brady says.

"Oh c'mon, don't sell yourself short. Intelligence isn't only studying at school and getting all A's on your assignments. It's creativity, it's growth and contribution, it's about being your authentic self! Anybody would be blessed to have you by their side."

"Like you?" Brady smirks.

"Yes, like me." I lean in for a kiss and we practically fall into each other.

Later we are ready to go out to grab some Thai food for lunch.

"You know," he says, "I've always wondered when you came out?"

"As a gay man?"

"Yeah."

"I was pretty lucky," I say. "I've always known I was gay."

"Seriously?" he asks, "even as a little kid?"

"Well, even as a little kid I always knew that I was different from the other kids, I just didn't have a name for it. It wasn't until I was about nine years old that I first heard the term *homosexual* and all the negative things that implied. I remember my parents taking me to church and hearing the pastor rail against it, how all homosexuals were going to hell! You know, the usual bullshit. I remember asking my mother what homosexuals were, and she told me they were boys who liked other boys instead of girls. I remember thinking *but, that's me!*"

"Did your parents freak out when you told them?"

"My mother cried. Then she told me that it was best that *she* told my father because we were both afraid of the way he would react to that bit of news."

"You mean he might have hit you?"

"We were both afraid of that type of reaction, for sure."

"Did she tell him?"

"I don't know. If she did, you would have never known it. Everything between us remained the same. No difference."

"Did you ever find out if your dad knew or not?"

"I never asked him, although I was sure that he knew. Funny though, it seemed little by little we became a little closer, until I decided to come to Canada to escape the draft."

"He was pretty pissed off with you?"

"Yeah. They didn't like it when I left."

"Did you come up here alone?"

"No, I came up with a couple of buddies of mine I knew from San Francisco. We'd heard that Vancouver in British Columbia was pretty much like San Francisco North, and it was easy to get here. Just go up to Seattle and then pop over the border no muss, no fuss."

"It wasn't really that easy, was it?"

"It was fairly easy because I already knew a couple of folks who were already here. I contacted them before I left San Fran, and they were waiting for me when I got off the bus in Vancouver. I stayed with them for a couple of years, and in the meantime, they helped to set me up to stay here at least until the draft was ended in the United States."

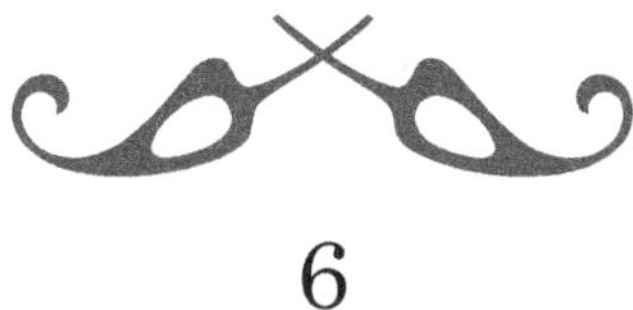

6

Lunch has become my favourite meal of the day. Brady and I sit at a Thai restaurant on Denman while we continue to catch up. We're listening to what I would describe as *Thai Pop* music over the sound system. We've ordered an appetizer and are quietly studying the menu because we had a toke before we got dressed and left the apartment, so now we both have the munchies and are focussed on our main course!

Brady chuckles.

"What's so funny?"

"Conrad," he snickers.

"Ah yes, Conrad..."

He's the live-in manager of our building, and the guy is on-call 24/7. He's a real jack-of-all-trades maintaining that building, and understandably, it can get frustrating for him sometimes.

Just as we were leaving to come here for lunch, Conrad was trying to intervene in a dispute between Charlie and Wayne, two old guys that have lived in the building for what seems, forever. These guys are infamous in our building, and they're the butt of many jokes. They're best friends and worst enemies, there have even been rumours they're actually a couple, but I've not seen anything that would substantiate that. They do, however, fight like a married couple, having had very public spats ever since I've lived in this building. Their apartments are beside each other on the main floor just off the lobby, and stories of their spats go back about twenty years or more, depending on who it is you're talking to in the building.

So, the two of them were out in the lobby, having yet another spat for the building to see, and the energy level was high while Conrad was trying to diffuse the situation and rapidly losing his patience.

"You're just a fuck-up!" Wayne pointing an accusing finger to Charlie.

"It wasn't me blarin' Arsehole Sam all damn morning!" shouted Charlie.

"It's not Arsehole Sam, it's Frankie Yankovic! *You're* Arsehole Sam! And you wouldn't know good music if it slapped ya in the arse!"

"Like hell I'm Arsehole Sam! YOU ARE!"

"NO! YOU ARE!"

"NO! YOU ARE!"

By this time, they were both yelling in unison to each other.

"YOU ARE!"

"YOU ARE!"

"YOU ARE!"

"YOU ARE!"

"NO! YOU ARE!" Charlie pointed his ass toward Wayne and ripped a fart.

"Did you see that!" Wayne to Conrad. "Did you see what he did? That old bugger's been doing that to me ALL DAMN MORNING!!"

"I HAVE NOT YA A-HOLE!"

"YOU'RE THE A-HOLE!"

"WILL YOU GUYS GROW UP!" yelled Conrad.

Charlie and Wayne were stunned silent, but only momentarily.

"We don't need to take that," Charlie said indignantly.

"Damn rights we don't," Wayne agreed. "Come into my place for a beer, Charlie."

The two entered Wayne's flat and just before Wayne shut the door, he turned to Conrad, pointing. "*You're* Arsehole Sam!" And slammed the door, leaving Conrad alone in the hall gritting his teeth.

He saw the two of us. "Why do I put up with this shit," he grumbled, "*especially* from *those* two!"

Brady still thinks it's hilarious as he chuckles.

He reaches across the table and puts his hand on mine. "That is wicked weed that we smoked by the way. You always did have the best pot."

"Thanks."

Then, Brady hands me a business card.

Brady Morgan Hempworth.

"Your last name's Hepworth! When did you decide to add the *m*?"

"You know me and pot."

"You amaze me, my boy. Speaking about toking, I've gotta remember not to get too stoned or I won't be able to read at the library tonight."

"Oh, why not? And who knows..." –Brady grins– "it might be funny as all get-out!"

"Yeah, right."

Brady looks out the window to the passing pedestrian traffic, then turns his attention back to me. "So, tell me about publishing this book."

"Where do you want me to begin?"

"Well, how do you feel about it?"

"What do you mean?"

"I know that was a labour of love for you..."

"Yeah..."

"Did you ever feel like it was *your* book instead of Warren's?"

"Hmmm. You know, it *did*. In many ways, it felt like *my* book, even though I knew it was his. The amount of work I put into organizing and putting all his diary outtakes and letters together in one, coherent volume. Then keyboarding it all and filling in the gaps as much as I could remember was a big task."

"I admire you for doing that."

"Thank you," I say. "But I probably would have done all this even if Warren *hadn't* asked me to. I knew it was something he wanted the world to remember him by."

"Who designed the cover?"

"The graphic designer at the publisher did, and I really like it." The book's cover features an aerial photo of downtown Vancouver which was taken about 1990 with Warren's name and the book title in yellow block lettering. It's quite impressive.

The waiter appears, puts the hot, deep fried spring rolls that we ordered on the table, refills our drinks, takes our main course orders, and disappears into the back once more.

Brady picks up a spring roll with his chopsticks, dips into the sauce that came with them and proceeds to eat. I, on the other hand, have never been an expert at the fine art of using chopsticks. So, I stab the roll with one stick and try to dip it in the sauce, only to have it collapse into the bowl. Brady chuckles.

"Still having trouble with those?" he asks.

"Some things just don't change I guess," I say trying to fish the now sticky and sopping end of the roll out of the bowl, giving up and using a fork instead.

"You know what I suddenly thought of?" Brady asks.

"What?"

"I remember you once told me about a guy you knew when you were growing up who lived like a hermit somewhere. Who was that?"

I have to think about that a moment as I take the first bite of my spring roll.

"Oh, Digger!" I say. "He was an old family friend back in Hawaii. My mom's side of the family knew him from when he was younger. We would go to visit him on the big island sometimes. He lived just outside of a small town called Pepeekeo, on the east side of the big island, out in the back country."

"Was he from Hawaii?"

"Nah, he was originally from Nowheresville, Mississippi, because that's what he would tell anybody who asked him. Apparently, he had horrible childhood and he didn't like to talk about it, his family, or his life growing up. So, we barely knew anything about his background or how my mom's folks knew him."

"He always said Nowheresville was a place where the folks wasted too much time *fartin' in the cat's face.*"

"What?" Brady laughed "What the hell is *that* supposed to mean?"

"I don't know. I think he made it up. But the way he would often use it, it would sound like it would mean when you're wasting time or goofing off. As my grandfather would say, someone like that would be a good-for-nothin' *layabout.*"

"When did you last see Digger?"

"Before I flew to San Francisco to go to university. I took the fifty-minute flight from Honolulu to the Big Island to see him for one last long weekend."

"*Last* long weekend?"

"Yeah, I kinda knew that was probably going to be the last time I'd ever see the old bugger, because he was pretty old at that time."

"How *old* is old?" Brady smiles at me.

"Let's see, I think he was pushing eighty the last time I saw him. Anyway, whenever I'd visit, he made sure there was a supply of his homemade beer and venison from an axis deer that he'd have bagged. This time was no exception.

"I remember that first night, we were sitting on a couple of chairs outside of his little place, in the dark after dinner. I remember that we were staring up to the night sky, and he had an old Billie Holiday LP on his record player. He was particularly animated after the two of us consumed a few beers each. He told me that he had seen a UFO land not too far from him only a couple of nights earlier."

I can still recall that conversation.

> "Are you sure you weren't drinkin' some of your home brew beforehand?" I asked.
>
> "Yah, up yours too," he said sporting a grin. "Hey, listen, it was in the middle of the night before last."
>
> His hands were shaking he was so excited.
>
> "The light from it was so bright It woke me up. Ya shoulda seen it! I looked out the windah, and all I seen were these four real bright lights, slowly comin' down from the sky and

landin' behind that grove of trees over there." He pointed at small grove of palm trees, and a small field beyond it.

"Theys demons," he said emphatically. "Demons I tells ya. They ain't mentioned in the Bible, so theys up ta no good!"

"When you saw it land, what did you do?" I asked him.

"I jes' stared at it for a while cuz I wasn't sure what to do. Then I sees this white light bein' shone from that flyin' machine to a spot not too far away. Then it goes out, and I ain't sure what's goin' on. All of a sudden I sees something comin' towards my place. Looked like three little people."

"Wow! What did you do then?"

"Well by this time I'm pissed off cuz I don't want no one comin' onta my land."

"So, what did you do?"

"I grabbed my rifle, put on my boots and ran buck-assed naked out the door towards them, yellin' my fool head off and firing off a few rounds while I was goin'!"

I saw clearly in my mind, what that must have looked like, and chuckled.

"Oh, yeah? Y'think it's funny, d'ya?" he asked half seriously.

"You running naked outside yellin' like an animal, and firing a rifle? Yeah, that's funny!"

He looked at me and a smirk cut across his face then he chuckled as well.

"Yeah, I s'pose it is."

"So, what did the Martians do then?" I asked him.

"Heh-heh, ya should seen them critters retreat! It looked like they jumped back about three steps and then it looked like they got sucked back inta that flyin' machine straight back ta Hell! *Heh-heh!*"

"You scared the shit out of them didja?"

"Yer damn rights! None of them critters is comin' onta my land. I don't care how smart they thinks they is!"

I relate all this to Brady, who eats it up along with his spring rolls.

"Amazing."

"Yeah, I haven't thought about old Digger for quite a while. I'll always be grateful to him."

"Why's that?" Brady asks.

"He was a fantastic guitar player, and anytime I went over there he would take it out and play."

"What did he like to play?"

"Mostly old blues, especially Robert Johnson and Billie Holiday. He was the guy who inspired me to eventually become a musician. I wanted to become as good as him on the guitar. So, when I was younger, I told him that, and when I was fourteen years old, he gave me his old guitar and started giving me lessons."

"Is that the guitar that's in the corner of the living room?"

"That's the one."

"It's a beautiful instrument."

"I'm blessed to have it. Anytime I play it, I think of Old Digger."

Then the rest of our meal arrives, and we quietly eat.

7

It's interesting that Brady would reappear in my life at this point. I have been thinking about him a lot lately, and now, voilà, here he is! Coincidence? As Warren used to say, "ain't it funny how life works sometimes?" I agree, and it's also a reminder of some of the things that have been happening to me lately, not physically, but inside of me, spiritually.

In my world, there's no such thing as coincidence. When my thinking of Brady seems to cause him to appear—well, it's almost like a prayer has been answered. Like some weird cosmic ear has heard my heart as it cries out and the Universe has put something in front of me to give me a sign that everything is okay—that I will be alright. A lot of this spiritual outlook I've adopted since my trip to New Zealand.

While Brady is in the bedroom having an after-lunch nap, I look at the koru that was given to me while I was in New Zealand. I found it while looking for something else in the bottom drawer of my dresser cabinet earlier this morning.

Before there was Brady, there was Paul. I got to know Paul not too long after I arrived in New Zealand. I found myself in a pub in Queenstown on the South Island, when this devilishly handsome and confident younger man with a trimmed beard, an illuminating smile, and dazzling brown eyes asked if he could sit with me.

"I'm Paul," he said reaching across the table to shake my hand.

"Daryl," I answered.

"Nice accent," he added, "You American?"

"Canadian."

"So, you're new here too."

I smiled. "Yes, just visiting. You're not from here?"

"Newcastle, England."

"Cool. Nice to meet you, Paul."

"Good to meet you too."

I've thought of Paul from time to time. I thought I was in love with him. Who am I kidding, of course I was! I could have stayed with him for the rest of my life. Like Brady—and Warren before him—he was younger than me, he was funny, intelligent, and kind (animals that we would encounter on our travels would take an instant liking to him, just like I did).

I travelled throughout New Zealand with him for two months as we explored both islands. We saw some great sights and met some amazing people. He loved to be naked as much as he could. I remember the first time he disrobed I admired the tattoos of birds all over his body. He loved birds.

"Birds are amazing creatures," he'd say. So, we both were naked as much as we could get away with it. As a result, we literally fucked our way throughout New Zealand. In hostels, fields, by riversides, hillsides, on beaches, you get the picture.

He made me feel special. Whenever I spoke to him, he would listen, I mean really listen to me. He would focus on me when I spoke, and ask me questions about my thoughts, my experiences, and my life in general. After we were travelling together for about a month, he started calling me his *tāne*, which is Māori for man/husband. That *really* made me feel special.

As I say, Paul was a very spiritual man, not in a traditional Abrahamic-Judeo-Christian sense, his beliefs were a mixture of Buddhism, traditional Māori and Native North American spirituality, Nature Worship, and some New Thought thrown in for good measure. Every morning he would wake up and say *Thank You* three times to the Universe/God. In fact, before and after he did most things, he would raise his hands, palms-up and loudly give thanks for all there is and for all he was given.

From Cape Reinga on New Zealand's northern tip to its southern tip at Stewart Island, I remember naked swims in the Tasman Sea at Hokitika, half-naked hikes around Milford Sound and Queenstown, talking with a Māori elder after he sang to the giant kauri trees on the North Island, and a guided tour that included a scary helicopter ride right into the actively volcanic Whakaari (a.k.a. White Island). It was Paul's idea to visit there.

"Mmm, I don't know…" I hesitated when he asked me to go with him.

"C'mon, we'll be fine," he answered. "It will be so cool to feel the raw energy of Mother Earth. Besides, the volcano won't hurt you and me, I promise."

"How can you promise *that?*" I asked.

"My prayers are strong," he answered. "Just wait, you'll see. We'll be fine."

So, we boarded the helicopter, flew forty-five kilometres out to sea, and descended right into an opening of the wall of the crater of this active volcano. It has been known to come alive quite suddenly. In fact, it has erupted continually since 1975. There was a sulphur mine on this Island up until the 1930s—even though in 1914 part of the crater collapsed killing ten miners. I remember the overwhelming stench of sulphur, as we got out of the helicopter while a moonscape with yellow sulphur deposits up the side of the crater walls surrounded us. As we walked along the surface, there was steam in the air, and I could feel the ground actively vibrating beneath my feet. Was I scared shitless being there? Damn straight I was! But I have to admit, it was an interesting experience that has stayed with me until this day. And Paul was right, the volcano never even emitted so much as a small burp while we were there. But we really got up-close-and-personal with the raw energy of Mother Earth, and that was both terrifying and mind-blowing all at the same time.

While we were on the north island, I noticed the Māori elder—the one who sang to the kauri—was wearing a jade koru. It looked like a large, green, spiral. I asked him the significance of it, and he told me that, to the Māori People, the silver fern is a spiritual symbol. The koru represented the young silver fern just as it uncoils and opens itself to Creation. Therefore, it signified an individual's spirit as it opened itself to all of Creation. I loved the concept and the look of the koru, and later I told Paul I wanted to get one. He told me that probably the best place for me to get one was in Hokitika on the South Island because I could get a genuine koru created by a Māori artist.

When we eventually arrived in Hokitika, it hadn't been two hours when Paul put a beautiful, jade koru around my neck and kissed me. He gave me the small box for it. Inside the box was an online link that I could click and see a photo of the piece of jade from where the koru was made, and the bio and photo of the Māori artist who carved it. I was blown away—first of all, I loved the fact that he bought it for me. Secondly, because it was made of jade, it was likely expensive. Thirdly, because I could see and read about the artist who carved it.

He smiled when I thanked him for it.

"It's only money, and you're not allowed to take money or possessions with you when you leave this Earth."

That was one of the most wonderful things that anybody had ever done for me.

Like me, he had his guitar with him and the two of us would play every evening. He loved Bob Marley, and we would play his songs a lot. He especially loved the song "One Love."

Well, all good things come to an end, and it ended with Paul when I told him I was in love with him. He was silent and only smiled at me, which I thought was a rather odd reaction. Then, a couple of days later, he told me that we would be parting company soon. I was stunned! What didn't occur to me at the time was that Paul wouldn't be tied down. After the fantastic couple of months of sharing laughs, making love, the travelling together, the singing and snuggling together every night, he was about to up and leave me.

"Why? Was it something I said? Something I did?"

"Daryl," he said, "I love you, and I've had a really fantastic time with you. But I need to be free to wander for as long as I can. I want to go place to place, meet new people, and have new experiences. That is not going to happen for me if I'm tied down in one place. What we had was amazing, and you're an amazing man. But the summer is almost over, and it won't be long before the winter winds will be here and—"

"I'll go with you. I wouldn't mind travelling with you at all."

He silently shook his head *no*.

"I don't understand."

"I don't expect you to," he answered. "What we had was fun, Daryl. You just need to accept that I'm not what you're looking for. I'll never make you happy."

"Strange, you've done a damn fine job of it these past couple of months."

"That wasn't me," he said, "that was *you* choosing to be happy, and choosing to come along for the ride. That was *you* opening yourself up to all the possibilities that life *can* offer you during our time together. And like everything else in the world, it all comes to an end."

"You know *that's* cold comfort," I said with a sarcastic tone.

"Look, I get it, you don't understand," he said, "but believe me, you'll move past this, and you'll move on."

"So, tell me, all this time that you've been calling me your tāne, that was all bullshit, wasn't it? You really didn't mean it, did you?"

"No, it wasn't bullshit. I really meant it."

"How could you call me your man, your husband and then in a twinkling, just up and leave me? What did I do that was so wrong?"

"You have to understand, Daryl, you did nothing but be your own wonderful self, and I love you for that, and I always will. Please try to understand, I'm a lone wolf. I'm sorry, but when you told me you wanted to stay with me… well… I can't do that."

"You *can't*, or you *won't*."

"Okay, it's both. I can't, so I won't. I do much better on my own. That's me, and it's time for me to move on. I live my life for me, Daryl. We've had a wonderful time together, and I'll always remember you. When I get together with somebody, like I have been with you, I give them my all. But like everything else in life, those relationships are only temporary. Eventually, it's time for me to move on."

I was silent for a moment then sighed sadly. "I guess there's nothing left for me to do but accept this." Then after a moment's silence, I asked. "Where are you going to go?"

"I'm going to meet some friends in Hanoi," he said. He paused then, sensing my sadness. "I'm sorry, Daryl. You're a sweet man, and I know that you'll find somebody else someday. I don't think you would be happy spending your life with me anyway."

"How would you know that?"

"I've spent enough time with you to know that you're the marrying type. You want to have a happy and stable relationship, and you *will* find that… just not with me. I'm not into that. Now, having said that, I can't speak for next year, the next five, or even the next ten years! But I do know that, right now, something's calling me to move on, and I have to be true to who I am and answer that call."

I felt overwhelming sadness enveloping me even more and my face must have shown it.

"Don't be sad, Daryl. Be happy for the time we've had together. You *will* find somebody who wants the same things as you do… and you'll find him when you return to Canada."

"How do you know that?"

"I just know. Believe me, I know. This man is going to be younger than you, handsome, intelligent, and bright. You two will instantly fall for each other."

Well, he was right about that. I smile and look toward the bedroom where Brady's napping.

The day that I watched Paul take his place in line to go through security at the Auckland Airport, I somehow knew that would be the last time I would ever see or hear from him. I felt the same kind of loneliness set in as after Warren died.

It was later that night, while I was sitting alone at a pub near the hostel where I was staying downtown, I heard a song on the jukebox, and all I could remember was the chorus, *"For today, I remember your smile."* I thought of Paul, and I thought of Warren, and despite the loneliness I was feeling, I liked the song. It was upbeat and happy.

I asked a group of partyers at a nearby table if they knew who was playing that song. They listened to a little bit of it over the din if the pub.

"Oh mate," said one of the guys, "that's an old song!"

"I've never heard it before," I answered.

"You're Canadian, aren't you?" asked one of the women.

"Well, yeah, I am," I answered.

"Canadian accents are so cool," said another woman.

I chuckled and thanked her.

"That song's by a group from Dunedin called Netherworld Dancing Toys," said the guy who first spoke. "It's called 'For Today'."

"Just like the chorus," I said.

"It was a big hit here a long time ago," said a third woman, "back about 1985, I think."

"You here alone?" asked another of the guys.

"Yes," I answered.

"Why don't you join us?"

"Thank you," I said as I pulled my chair over to join them.

After introductions and some small talk, I found out that a couple of the guys were in a band, and, strange though it was, we all bonded that evening. I had so much in common with them it was like I found my peers. I ended up hanging out with them for the remainder of my time there. We would jam and sing a lot, and I was even invited to perform with them a couple of times at their gigs. I headed down to Wellington with them, and we spent our time between there and Nelson on the South Island. I've kept in touch with them over the years, and I would never have met them had Paul not left me, and I ended up in that pub.

"Ain't it funny how life works sometimes?" I couldn't agree more, Warren. I couldn't agree more.

8

It's a bit later in the day, and as Brady and I are out for an afternoon walk. I'm silent as my mind drifts and he senses it.

"What are you thinking about?"

"I was just thinking about an incident that took place not long after Warren found out he was HIV positive."

"And what was that?"

"Well, I don't know what's made me think about this, but one night I arrived home after a gig to find Warren slumped on the couch. He still had his coat and shoes on and was staring at the ceiling. He was motionless, like he was transfixed on the ceiling fan."

"Was he stoned."

"Yes, but not blissfully so. I knew that he had been out to his old roommate's place."

"Was that Don?"

"Yeah, Don and his boyfriend Jerry had invited him to dinner over at their place that evening. He was looking forward to it because it was the first time he'd seen Don since he moved in with me."

"I remember saying, 'Hey, what's happening?' as I took off my coat. But he didn't respond. 'How was dinner with Don and Jerry?' He glanced at me but remained silent. That's when I knew something was up."

"What happened?"

"He sat up, unbuttoned his jacket and slowly took it off, and for the first time, I noticed that he had lost some weight that he couldn't afford to lose. That startled me."

"I remember you saying that, once the illness took hold, he went pretty fast," Brady says.

"Yeah, it was a little over two years after his original diagnosis." I fall silent for a few moments, then continue. "Anyway, back to the story… he gave me this really sad look."

"'They don't want nothin' to do with me no more,' he said, and I remember sitting beside him on the couch and asking him what happened?"

"He told me that everything was going along great, they were having fun and talkin' about old times. They'd already had a few glasses of wine, and the three of them had a couple of tokes. Then, after dinner they started talking about AIDS and HIV. I guess that Jerry started being all high and mighty saying shit like, those who got it, deserved it. And he had no sympathy for gay guys like that."

"You're fucking kidding me," Brady says.

"That's what Warren told me. Apparently, Warren got a little pissed at Jerry and asked, what he meant by *gay guys like that?*"

"What did Jerry say?"

"According to Warren, Jerry got really mouthy and started going on about how faggots have no morals, and they need to learn to be more conventional and more accepting to the general public."

"I hope that Warren told him that he was full of shit!" Brady snorts.

"He did."

"What did they do?"

"I guess that Don was quiet, but Jerry got started going on about how the gay community has to learn to be moral and quit being a bunch of sluts, and he kept going on about how guys who got HIV deserved it. That's when Warren got really pissed off and told them he was HIV positive."

"What did they do?"

"Apparently, Jerry demanded to know how long he'd known, and Warren told him that he had only found out a couple of months before. I guess the two of them went really quiet."

"Did they actually tell him they didn't want anything more to do with him?"

"Yeah, they did. I guess that Jerry told Warren that and he and Don thought it best he leave their place and not come back."

"Jesus Christ. Why?"

"Warren told me it was because he was HIV, and they didn't want him near them anymore."

"What? Didn't they know that they could only be exposed to it if they had unprotected sex with them both?"

"That's what he told them."

"What did they say?"

"He said it was like Jerry didn't even hear him. He started telling him all kinds of shit like how he knew that Warren was always a bad roommate to Don and how he was totally irresponsible. That if he hadn't been such a slut then maybe he wouldn't be sick."

"That prick," Brady swears. "Didn't Don say anything in his defence?"

"Apparently not."

Brady's silent for a moment.

"Was there really that kind of divide in the Queer Community back then?"

"There were some in the gay community that discriminated against those who seroconverted, which was the term used for when somebody went from being HIV negative, to positive. That kind of discrimination didn't happen a lot, but it happened."

"So, what happened after that?"

"Apparently, just before he put on his coat and went out the door, Warren told Jerry that he was nothing but a mouthpiece! And Don was nothing but a coward. He told me that he said, 'No wonder you ain't got no fuckin' friends, and you know that's true. Fuck you guys!' I guess that Jerry yelled at him to get out just as Warren was leaving."

"Warren said he slammed their door as he left."

"I don't blame him."

"When he got home, he sat on the couch wondering if this was the way things were going to be. He wondered if he could expect this kind of abuse from other gay guys for the rest of his life. I mean, Warren thought that he and Don were good friends."

"Were you able to offer him any kind of encouragement?"

"I was at a loss as to what to tell him. The poor guy was obviously crushed because of this. I cuddled him close and told him that I didn't know what's going to happen. I told him that Jerry and Don were jerks, and what they did to him said more about them than it did about him. But I also told him that I thought the gay community was gaining enough knowledge and strength about HIV and that he was going to find a lot more support and friendship in the gay community, than adversity.

"I told him to think of the friends he was making through his volunteer work at the at BCPWA. So, you lost a couple of guys you thought were good friends, I told him, and as it turns out, they were nothing but shitheads. And you know what? Yeah, it hurts right now, but they've made it clear that they were never his friends in the first place. What kind of a person kicks a friend when they're down? What kind of a friend judges another friend when he's in need? He didn't need their judgements, or their snooty pettiness. Fuck them! I didn't think much of those two anyway. They were phonies, especially that Jerry. And I reminded him that he seemed to like the folks over at BCPWA, and he'd probably make a lot more good friends there. They've done you a favour by tossing you out of their lives."

"What did he have to say that?"

"It was actually funny. He said the only thing Jerry and Don would ever get will be the Joan Crawford Shoulder-Pads-and-Wire-Hanger Award for the Bitchiest Performance of the Decade!"

Brady bursts out laughing.

"It's getting late," I say. "Maybe we should be getting back to my place and think about a little bit of dinner before we head out to the library."

"Still got the munchies from that wicked weed?" Brady asks.

"I guess I do."

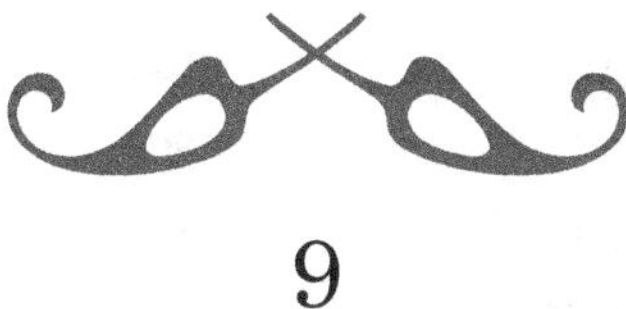

9

"How long did you live in San Francisco?" he asks as we head back to my place.

And he has asked this before, I am sure. I think he likes hearing me talk. Not a bad trait in a partner.

"A couple of years."

"Is what I've heard about it back in those days true?"

"That depends on what you've heard."

"About the open gay scene and sex everywhere."

"Yeah, all of that was certainly happening," I say. "That was the reason I left Honolulu to go to U of C Berkley. Not only did it have a reputable music program, but I'd heard about the things going on in the city, and I wanted to experience the burgeoning gay scene. It was the early seventies, and all the hippies were slowly moving on to other areas of the state, and the time was right for us gays and lesbians to move in and take over, if you will. Pretty much the same thing was happening up here in Vancouver at the time."

"I wish I could have been part of all that. I feel like I was born too late. Did you know anybody that you could have stayed with in San Francisco?"

"Yeah, I knew a guy named Tom who I met while he was on vacation in Hawaii. We fucked around then and kept in touch. When I told him that I had been accepted to the University of California Berkley, he told me that he had an extra room he could rent me at his place. So at least I didn't have to worry about finding a place to live."

"Did you feel any earthquakes while you were there?"

"Yeah, the first night I arrived actually." And I know I have told this story before. "Tom and I were up talking and went to bed about midnight. We hadn't been in bed fifteen minutes when a little shaking happened. It didn't last very long but it did startle me."

"Wow! My only time to San Francisco I remember rainbow flags everywhere, especially on Castro Street."

"When I was there in the early seventies, it was the pink triangle and the lambda symbol that were everywhere."

"No rainbow flags?"

"They didn't appear until about 1978, and when they did, it seemed the lambda and pink triangle disappeared completely."

"I know about the Nazis and what pink triangle meant," Brady says. "But what's the lambda?"

"It's a part of the Greek alphabet, and it kind of looked like an upside-down Y. The Gay Movement adopted it as the symbol of gay liberation in the late sixties and early seventies."

"Why?"

"Because it was seen as a symbol which meant balance and enlightenment; therefore, it was a perfect symbol to represent the same rights for gay people and straights."

Brady has taken out his smart phone and quickly peruses the text on his phone "Here it is… *in the 1970s, it became an international symbol of gay liberation and a modern symbol of their struggle, especially after Stonewall…* Cool! So, tell me some more about what you remember."

"I do remember some things, but a lot it is a blur, mostly because of the partying that I did."

"Like what do you remember?"

"I remember my favourite restaurant at the time was called It's Tops Coffee Shop on Market Street near Octavia. It seemed my friends and I were always there. So, great for breakfast in the morning after we'd been out partying all night. And I remember my best buddy, Hugo Gonzalez and I always were arriving there after all-nighters, both studying and partying. We all called him Speedy. At that time, he had bought a new Chevy Camaro SS Coupe, and whenever he'd drive, he'd floor the gas pedal, yelling, ándele, ándele… like Speedy Gonzalez on Bugs Bunny."

"You guys were close?"

"We called ourselves the Sisters of the Night! I met him after I'd been in San Francisco for a couple of weeks. Actually, we had met at an after-hours pub called the End Up. It was pretty notorious as an after-hours place and famous for hosting fundraising events for the community."

"And that's where the Sisters of the Night hung out?"

"Pretty much." I let out a sigh, feeling heavy hearted.

"What is it?"

"Ahhh just thinking of Hugo again makes me a little sad. I haven't thought about him for years, and I had wondered if he's still around."

"You lost touch?"

"I did. The last I heard, he wasn't well at all. But there's no way that I could verify any of that. You know, my decision to resist the draft feels like a chapter in my life there's no closure to."

"How do you mean?"

"A lot of my family wanted nothing to do with me after that, and I've lost touch with so many of the friends I had at that time, and I suspect many are gone from AIDS. For a few years after I left the States, there was no way I could return because it would mean jail time for me, and so—"

"But you told me you don't have to face that anymore because of there was an amnesty, right?"

"That's true," I said, "back in '77, and I did think seriously about going back and starting all over again when it was announced, but it just didn't feel right for me to be doing that. So, I remained up here and am grateful to be in Canada. I would rather be here than anywhere in my home country right now."

"I'm glad you've decided to stay, Papi," Brady says putting his hand over mine.

I look at Brady, smile, and clasp his hand. "I'm glad I made that decision too."

"Were there any great hiking places around San Francisco?"

"Speedy and I used to like to hike around Point Reyes, which was about an hour and a half north the city. He'd blast the radio, rev the Camaro and away we'd go! The hiking was great, and a lot of it was very long and tiring. Then there were times we'd drive out to Drakes Beach, which wasn't too far from Point Reyes, and it was windy a lot of the time. It was also close to a hamlet called Inverness where we would sometimes have dinner at a Czechoslovakian restaurant, I forget the name, but the food was great though quite expensive, and the waiter could be really abrasive sometimes. I don't know why they kept him on staff."

"Maybe he was part of the attraction."

"Ya never know."

We were quiet for a moment then. It felt good to be holding hands.

"I remember when I was in class at U of C Berkeley, Speedy would drive over to have coffee with me in the campus coffee shop. There was always a group of us who'd meet there, and we'd get into conversations about the merits of free enterprise versus socialism, the Vietnam War versus the peace movement, and I remember one night we were talking about Native American rights in the US, and things got a little tense."

"Why was that?"

"Well, at the time, members of the American Indian Movement had occupied Alcatraz Island."

"Wow. Was that a protest?"

"It was more of a reclamation that had begun a couple of years before. The idea was supposed to be to let the American public know the plight of Native Americans and for them to assert their need for self-determination."

"Why did things get a little testy at coffee that night?"

"Unfortunately, at this point, AIM was losing support among the general public. I guess the occupation went on for so long that people were tired of it, or worse yet, indifferent. Some of the people on campus were a little less than sympathetic, in fact, some seemed to be a little hostile toward them."

"How so?"

"Well, that night this one guy was sayin' shit like *they were conquered and should just learn to accept their place in society*. Of course, I didn't agree and let him know in no uncertain terms. Which led to things getting tense that night."

"Why would he say shit like that?"

"I don't know, but what I found the most surprising and disappointing about this was that it was coming from a member of the faculty that had joined us. After he said that, I openly questioned his integrity as an instructor, and that didn't go over so well."

"Sounds like he deserved it."

"He definitely did! And what further surprised me was that he was gay, and a real gay liberationist at that. I felt that he should know better than to make judgements on other people if he didn't want others to make judgements on us. And that's what I told him!"

"That's when things got tense?"

I nod. "Yeah, that's when he was getting verbally abusive to me. So, I got assertive and claimed he had no right to be a gay liberationist if he was denigrating other segments of society. He was being a hypocrite and the word of a hypocrite should never be believed!"

I look at Brady and smile. "I don't think he liked that."

"No, I wouldn't think so," Brady said. "What happened next, did he storm off?"

"He might have but Speedy, who was speedy in lots of ways, was already on his feet and making noise about being in the mood for chowder, and the next thing I knew we were climbing into the Camaro and heading to Fisherman's Wharf."

"So, he really did want chowder."

I smile at that. "Sure. Probably. I mean, Sabello & LaTorre was easily our *second* favourite restaurant. It might have been our number one if it opened for breakfast and served pancakes. We'd often hit it for lunches on Friday afternoons. It was a funky little place that was half restaurant and half bar. There were always fresh prawns and crabs being sold on-ice just outside the main entrance, so we'd have a fresh seafood lunch and get a little pie-eyed."

"You know, I think I might have been there."

"Maybe you were," I say. "It's kind of a San Francisco institution. It's funny, I remember this one time Speedy and I were sitting at the bar and had just started our first beer when we got talking to two straight couples sitting at the bar near us. They had just flown in from Chicago, and the two women were feeling no pain though the two guys seemed to be pretty lucid. Apparently, the gals started drinking on the plane and were kind of loud, but they were happy drunks, the two of them were laughing and joking. The two guys were the ones doing most of the talking, in fact, they took a real interest in us."

"How so?"

"As soon as the women went to the washroom together, they came over to us and began talking to us directly. Speedy and I both instinctively knew they probably clued in that we're gay and wanted some action."

"And did they?"

"Yeah, they sure did. The women returned and wanted to go back to the hotel. So, the guys gave them cab fare and told them they weren't ready to go back to the hotel yet. After the women were gone, they told Speedy and me they had been fucking each other for a couple of years and liked to get away to *play with the boys* occasionally. After lunch and a couple of more beer, we piled in Speedy's car, rented a room at a cheap motel near the Castro, and had a foursome with them for a couple of hours."

"DAMN! Sounds like it was fun back then."

"Well, we were young and cute, and into a good time." A shadow of something must cross my face because Brady catches it.

"What's the matter?"

"I miss Speedy. I've missed him for many years, and I'm sorry I lost touch with him."

10

We are back at my place—in the kitchen, now, as I throw together a quick pasta dish with prawns. It has to be quick because I have the reading coming up. It feels good to be keeping busy. Of course, the talk has turned to the book.

"So how was it that you took over finishing Warren's book?"

"Simple," I said, "Warren asked me to. I remember him saying, and this was very near the end as it turned out, he said, 'Fuck, I ain't gonna be the writer I was hopin' ta be.' And that broke my heart, so I tried to talk around it, y'know, but he wasn't having it.

"He just shook his head. 'Nah, I'm gonna be gone soon, and I just don't know if I'm gonna have the strength I need to pay much attention to putting it together no more. I need ya to help me finish it. And when the time comes for me to go, and it still ain't published, promise me you'll finish it and get it published for me.' What could I say?"

"That must have been a hard promise to keep, at first." says Brady.

"Yeah, inside I was scared. Firstly, because I didn't like to even think of him dying on me, and secondly because I didn't know if I would do this justice. But I said yes, and he said, 'I'll do what I can ta help ya out while I'm still here.' And to be fair, he did."

It was the beginning of a trip that would take the next few years to have an ending, or should I say, a new beginning.

I remember him saying that when he was in jail, they had to keep a daily journal. His probation officer would use that to track his progress while inside. It would also give the authorities a good idea as to his mental state at any given time. That practice got so drilled into him that he just kept up with the journaling long after he was released back to the community. He used them as the basis to write his book.

In the kitchen, the pasta is on the boil, so I open the book, and as I read to Brady, I could almost hear Warren's voice.

> "You know the day your baby boy will be born," Kookum said, "because the doves outside will not sing on that morning."
>
> "How do you know my baby will be a boy?" Mom asked.
>
> Kookum smiled and said, "I just know."
>
> That's how Kookum told me it happened.
>
> She said that a couple of weeks before I was born there were some doves that would sit in a tree outside of the house early every morning cooing.
>
> "Your mom wouldn't believe me when I told her this would happen, and it did. One morning the doves didn't come, and you were born that afternoon."
>
> I loved Kookum (she was my grandmother—that's what she always told me to call her because she said Kookum meant grandmother in Cree). She always loved me and showed it. She read to me when I was kid, sang to me before I went to bed at night, told me stories of our ancestors, made chocolate chip bannock for me, and gave me lots of hugs and kisses. Mom and Kookum always had a strange relationship. They fought a lot, but when they weren't fighting, they were like the best of friends.
>
> I didn't know a lot about my family, and what I did know, it was Kookum who told me. I remember Kookum telling me once that mom had run away to Edmonton from a residential school somewhere in Saskatchewan. But Kookum didn't know that until a couple of days later when my mom called her from Edmonton. All she would tell Kookum was that she went to Edmonton because she knew she could stay with her

cousin Phoebe's family, and there were lots of places to hide, so the authorities would have a harder time finding her there.

Government men showed up at Kookum's place a couple of times demanding to know where my mother was.

"But I told them I hadn't heard a word from her, and I was really worried. I even let them search my house every time, just to prove to them that she wasn't there."

"Kookum, isn't it wrong to tell a lie?" I asked.

She chuckled. "Yes, it is Little Muskwa. But I also knew that your mom wasn't happy at that school. And if I let them send her back to that place, she might not have ever forgiven me."

"Why, Kookum?"

"Because there were many stories about some of the things that were happening in there."

"Like what, Kookum?"

"We heard there were children being beaten for speaking their language, and there were some other bad things happening in those places."

"How come nobody stopped it?"

"These were only things we were hearing. Any time we would ask the government people about it, they always told us these things we heard were lies, and that the children were being well looked after. I always felt that it was the English people that were not telling us the truth. And for that reason, I knew that your mother was better off with her cousin Phoebe and her family in Edmonton.

"And besides," Kookum added, "the English men who came looking for your mom, didn't need to know where she was anyway. And when I found out your mom had met a guy and was pregnant, I went to Edmonton to be with her until after you were born."

We never saw much of my old man, and when he was around, all hell would break loose. I never knew much about him—except I hated the drunken fucker and didn't want to know anything about him.

We hardly ever had money to eat, I remember eatin' a lot of Kraft Dinner and fried bologna cuz that's all Mom could afford. And I remember he always had money to drink, even if that meant takin' it from Mom by beatin' on her and ransackin' the place to find any dollars she had hidden away. Any time I tried to stop him, I'd get a beatin'. I know that most of his family was from Ireland and that every one of them were big time fuckin' drunks too. I remember Mom and me movin' a lot, but the fucker would find us and be on our doorstep again."

I sometimes found the passages I was reading to be really difficult. From the time when he was a kid, he had to deal with a lot of shit that so many of us couldn't even imagine.

11

When I was putting Warren's book together this passage stood out for me, he dated it November 1989.

> Lately I've really been bitching to Daryl about feeling cold a lot. I've been wearing Mooshum's jacket with a sweater underneath it. It doesn't make any sense to me. I'm feeling cold all the time.

I remember back then, whenever I saw him feeling cold in the warm, summer weather, I'd go off alone and cry. I knew if he ever saw me crying about the state of his slowly failing health, he would be upset that I was upset.

Sometimes I felt like I couldn't go on, watching two people that I'd grown to love, Warren and Ma, slowly deteriorate. I felt so helpless. Still, the two of them kept me going. I swear the HIV diagnosis was giving him more resolve to get the most out of life he could. That fire that burned within him was getting stronger as the time went on. And I was happy it did, especially for him and Ma. It was like the strength he gained from that fire within, he was also giving to Ma, Phoebe, Hunter, and me.

He became passionate about his volunteer work with the BCPWA Society. He was one of the guys who would help with things like the annual walk-a-thon they would have to raise funds. He especially liked to help out at that event. I remember reading in Warren's notes that by 1988 the PWA Society were ready to add to their programs and they needed extra cash. The walk-a-thon that year raised $15,000 and the society's federal funding was increased to $50,000. That October, the City of Vancouver also kicked in almost $12,000 for its core funding. The BCPWA Society was gaining all kinds of strength, and it seemed to be rubbing off on him. He was really excited about that. It really gave him a sense of accomplishment to think he was part of that fundraising, and to be in on the ground floor of a budding organization.

I remember those experiences helped him grow, and he got to know the person he really was. The fact that he no longer had full time work meant that it got him out of the house and doing something he found fulfilling. He was working with people who shared his diagnosis, and I think for the first time in his life he could look in the mirror and say, Warren, you ain't such a bad shit after all. And that newfound self-assurance gained him attention in some big ways. He was becoming friends with a lot of the people there.

I'll never forget this one late afternoon… we had taken up our usual places at the Royal with a few of the other volunteers from the society. The Castle Pub had shut down the year before and now the Royal was the pub where the LGBTQ+ would gather. I went to the washroom and had stopped to talk to some buddies on the way back to the table. When I finally returned, there was a large piece of paper sitting on the table. Ma, Phoebe, and a few of the guys were admiring it. I looked at it, and it was a drawing of Warren.

"You should have seen what just happened," Phoebe said. "We were just sitting here when this guy came up to Warren and hugged him, then he gave him this piece of paper."

"It was Colin," said Warren with a big grin on his face. Colin was one of the other volunteers at BCPWA. "We've been talking to each other a lot lately."

"He told Warren that he always thought he was one of the handsomest and most interesting men he'd ever seen," Ma said beaming with pride. "And my baby *is* handsome." Then she leaned in pinching his cheek.

"Ah Ma, stop that!" he protested.

"Oh yeah," Phoebe said while reaching over to pinch his other cheek, "look at him, he's so cute."

"Cut it out," he protested a little louder but smiling all the while. That's when everyone around the table started. *Ohhhh he's so cute! Oohh, look at him!*

"Cut it out, guys!" he protested, still with a big grin on his face. We all laughed.

I picked up the paper for a closer look. It was a pencil sketch of Warren's profile as he appeared to be listening to somebody across the table from him. Part of Ma's face was directly behind him looking in the same direction. I could see where Colin had quickly sketched some of the crowd in the background, with the exit sign at the alley entrance hanging at the top of the page. The sketch was beautiful. It caught the two of them as they were, the looks on their faces, the smiles on their lips and the very shine in their eyes.

"We'll definitely get this framed and hang it in the living room," I said.

"That would be a good place for it," said Ma with a broad smile.

That sketch now hangs in my living room in plain view of anyone who enters.

12

One memory that will always remain with me was the evening that fall when Warren reconnected with his old friends Bert—Warren called him Gil—and Neil. I was so glad to see this because Warren would talk a lot about Bert and the time they spent in jail together back in Alberta. Bert was like the protective big brother that Warren never had. Somewhere on their journey inside, they became lovers too.

He once said to me, "Y'know, the biggest regret I have is fuckin' up my friendship with Gil."

I remember that night they reconnected. I was in the kitchen of our place doing the dinner dishes when the phone rang. I remember that call so well. I answered it.

"Hello."

"Um, hello, is Warren Givens there?'

"Yeah. Who's calling?"

"Bert Gilhuis from Toronto."

I called Warren and told him who it was. He ran upstairs from the basement, grabbed the phone from me, and was panting when he answered. "GIL! HOW THE FUCK ARE YA?! It's been sooo fuckin' long!"

Warren looked at me and gave me the thumbs up, just beaming. Finally, Warren connected with him after all this time. Good! Warren had all but had given up on ever hearing from Gil and Neil again.

"I'm doing great! You?" Warren said into the phone.

"Cool, what? Yeah, I got out about five years ago… well, you know me… what? Yeah, trying to keep my nose clean this time."

"You in Toronto? Cool. Is Neil still around? That's great! Tell him I say hello. Oh wow! You guys bought a house? Where? Where's Barrie? Why there? Oh, so you're close to Neil's folks. Fantastic!"

He chuckled like a little boy.

"What's that?" he asked. "You guys just bought a cottage too? Where's Muskoka? Huntsville? No, I never… Gravenhurst? No, ain't never heard of that place either. Oh, okay, central Ontario. Super! I'll bet you spend a lot of time up there, eh? Ah, every weekend in the summer… betcha it's great to get out of the city for a while?

"So how did you find out where to get hold of me? Oh. No, I don't know him personally, but I *have* heard our roommate mention him because he's his cousin. Is he a friend of yours? Oh, a friend of a friend, heh-heh, small fuckin' world, eh?

"Yeah Gil, I *have* been looking for ya. Y'see, there's a couple of things I need to tell ya.

"Well, first, I need to apologize for what happened the last time I saw ya. I really fucked things up and heard that you got hassled by the screws when you tried to see me at Vancouver Remand… WHAT? THEY STRIP SEARCHED YA? Oh, fuck man, I'm *really* fuckin' sorry, Gil. I had no idea that happened. Fuck! I should've listened to you and Neil before I went down to Wreck Beach that morning and—shit, Gil, I'm so sorry. No wonder you didn't want nothin' to do with me.

"No, it's not alright. You almost went back to fuckin' jail because of me. I hope that one day you can forgive me."

Then I remember him happily sighing.

"Ah thanks Gil. Yeah, life *is* too short.

"Do you… well, d'ya think we can call it friends again? … You still there, Gil? … Ah, thanks Gil. You always were a great pal. I'm so fucking sorry for what happened when we were on our trip together. That will always be the biggest regret of my life."

Then Warren was silent for a few moments.

"Yeah, there is something else I need to tell you. Well, uh... I have HIV. Yeah, that's right. So, I need to tell you so that you and Neil should go get tested and... oh... you guys have already been tested? Fuck, that's great! Yeah, thank Christ you're both negative. Well, thanks, but I suppose it was bound to happen sooner or later, Gil. Let's face it, I ain't never been no angel, and with me it's always been the-more-the-merrier.

"Yeah, I do, that's who answered the phone. His name is Daryl... yeah, he's a super guy." He turned and smiled at me.

I smiled back and blew him a kiss. He blew one back.

"No, no," he said into the phone. "I'm just blowing Daryl a kiss. Yeah," he chuckled again, "we'll be doing *that* kind of blowing later."

I could hear Gil laugh through the phone.

"What's that? Yeah, sure, I'd love to come down to see you guys again, but I'm not working full time anymore, so I have to watch my pesos.

"Hey Gil, you guys could come out here *anytime*, we've got room here for you two to crash. The Gay Games are next year! You guys could come out for that! Yeah, sure, I understand, you have to watch your pennies because you have a new house, but still...

"Yeah, it is something to think about. I would love to see you guys again, and you guys would love Daryl.

"Really? Yeah... please think about it, Gil. That would be great if you guys can do it. Let me know, okay?"

And after a little more catching up, Warren and Bert said their goodbyes.

The next of the nice surprises happened two days later when Bert called him back to say that he and Neil had been going over their finances and decided they would be coming out to the Gay Games after all. Warren was beside himself with excitement when Bert added they were going to make a holiday out of it, and they took Warren up on his offer to crash with us.

They told him they would drive out from Ontario, and I remember Warren told me that, according to Bert, Neil had pretty much driven that same trip back in 1979 with a friend of his who was a military officer. From what I understand, there were romantic intentions, but it didn't end well.

Warren was really looking forward to their arrival, and I was looking forward to meeting them. Things like this were good for Warren, they gave him reasons to get up the next day.

13

It was 1990 and there was excitement in the city leading up to the Gay Games; the hype was everywhere. It was in the newspapers, on the radio and television, on posters that were stapled, taped, and thumbtacked on every available space everywhere in this city and beyond. I got really excited at the thought of gay and lesbian athletes from all over the world coming here to Vancouver for ten days! It was the first time the Games had been held outside of the United States. Since then, it has gone to places like: Amsterdam, Cologne, Paris, and Sydney.

It had local religious types scared. A bunch of Christian pastors out in the Fraser Valley Bible Belt calling themselves the Watchmen for the Nations had taken a full-page ad in the local newspaper warning everyone that God would send an earthquake or some shit to swallow Vancouver whole if this *"sodomite invasion"* went ahead as planned. Even our Charismatic Catholic Premier at the time, Bill Vander Zalm, refused provincial government funding the event because homosexuality's against *his* religion. Never mind that government money is public money that *all* British Columbians contributed to. Goddamn I can't stand politicians and their overdeveloped, undeserved sense of privilege; they always piss me off!

As for that big earthquake that was going to happen… well, it didn't! I guess we humans just have admit that we have no say about what God is—or is not—going to do. Even though there are some who, motivated by their fears, like to *think* they do.

Anyway, it was one hell of a busy summer in this town. Because not only did Vancouver host the Third International Gay Games, but the first annual Molson 500 Indy Race, and the first Symphony of Fire brought hundreds of thousands of folks into the city *all around the same time*. It was crazy exciting!

I was in the Royal Pub one evening, waiting for Ma and Warren, and it was absolutely packed! I was starting to get concerned that they wouldn't be able to get into the pub because of fire regulations. Therefore, I knew there would be a huge line-up outside. I also knew that neither Warren nor Ma would be able to stand for long periods of time. I asked Peter, the head bouncer to be on the lookout for them.

Peter… it's been a while since I've thought of him, what a guy. He was a tall, handsome, well-muscled straight guy, who really liked to joke around with us patrons. He was always dressed in black jeans, black boots, a black leather bar vest, and he'd sometimes wear a white T-shirt with *Nobody Knows I'm a Lesbian* printed down the front of it. He especially loved to joke with Ma and Phoebe. They both thought he was really sexy (and he was)! He always stationed himself just inside the main entrance of the place, especially when they were anticipating a big crowd—which they usually were on the weekends.

Anyway, I was watching and listening to a couple of guys at a nearby table, and they were laughing at one of the big Gay Games posters on the wall. It featured two, big bear-like guys dressed like traditional Dutch women. The guys on the poster were not attractive and had makeup troweled on their faces while sporting facial hair and hand-sized eyelashes.

"Is that you on the right in that poster?" One of the giggling guys said to the other.

The other guy laughed and didn't say anything. I chuckled at that.

It was about seven o'clock, and I was slowly sipping my beer. A band called Snap! was singing "The Power" from the jukebox. Warren and I heard it a lot in those days, and we liked it, so we had the CD at home. The jukebox sat at the back wall by the men's washroom, and just beside a staircase that led up to the back exit to the alley.

I've always liked the Royal, right from the moment I walked in, it was packed, the energy in the room was over-the-top. Everything I was hearing about it was true. It was fun, and it was (almost) my second home. There were many guys who came up from Seattle and Portland who would say there was nothing like the Royal back home, so they really liked supporting it whenever they visited.

Anyway, as I was keeping watch for Ma and Warren, Terry, the bar's manager stood at my side holding his cigarette in his right hand while his other hand was tucked inside his pants pocket, as was his usual stance. He had been the manager of the Castle Pub, and when it shut down a couple of years before, he was instrumental at convincing the owners of the Royal to make *it* the new gay gathering place.

It was a decision they didn't regret because it was a popular gay hangout, and the opportunity was a goldmine for them. So, Terry ended up managing the Royal and brought a lot of the Castle staff with him.

Anyway, he smiled at me.

"You're here alone?" He said raising his voice to be heard over the din of the crowd and the music on the jukebox.

"Yeah," I yelled back to him. "Just waiting for the husband and Ma. They went to the afternoon showing of *Dances with Wolves*, I'm expecting them to arrive in a bit. I've got Peter looking out for them."

Silence led to small talk. "Hey Terry," I said, "is it true what I heard?"

"What did you hear?"

I point to a framed portrait of Queen Elizabeth hanging on a wall nearby. "That picture of the Queen… I heard that's the same picture that hung at the Castle."

"Yep, that's true enough."

"I heard a bunch of guys carried it from the Castle down Granville Street here to the Royal."

Terry chuckled. “Yep, I remember it well. It was the final day the Castle was open. I closed the bar early that day but let about ten of the regulars stay for one last drink. All the other patrons had come down here to the Royal before I locked the doors. Anyway, the bunch of them had one last pint together. Her Majesty had already been taken down from the wall, so I went and got it and gave it to Fraser, one of the guys still hanging around. All them got to hang onto their glasses as keepsakes, and when Fraser finished his pint, he took the portrait, raised it above his head, and started down the Granville Mall to the Royal here with the group following him.”

“That must have been a sight.”

“It was. I think that will probably go down as a pivotal moment in local gay history.”

“How so?”

“It was so proudly visible, carrying that portrait from one gay hangout to another so publicly was amazing. And the crowd on the Granville Mall went crazy when they saw the portrait coming. All the guys were singing *God Save the Queen* the whole time.”

“I heard there was a Scottish piper that was with you guys on Granville and piped the Queen into the pub here?”

“Nope, nothing like that. But the crowd in here went wild when they saw the portrait enter the pub. The old staff were still working at the time, and they were totally freaked out as the new patrons took over!”

“Amazing,” I said.

“So, are you going the Games?” Terry asked.

“What? Yeah, it’s gonna be great!”

“Got your tickets for any of the big events?”

“Not yet,” I said. “We’re hoping to get to both the Opening and the Closing Ceremonies.”

“It’s shaping up to be a big party. We’ve been making arrangements for extra staff for months now.”

“Yeah, I guess you guys are going to be run off your feet.”

“You got that right.”

"Do you guys have the entertainment roster ready to go for the time the Games are in town?" I asked.

Terry looked at me and smiled. "That's actually something I want to talk to you about. Would you be free for at least some of that week to play here?"

"I certainly can be," I answered.

"Can you put a band together for then?"

"Damn straight I can!"

"I'll be here every day this week. Why don't you pop in, and we can talk about it?"

"Fantastic!" I exclaimed. "How about tomorrow?"

"Tomorrow is good," Terry answered.

It was then I saw Peter standing at the entrance scanning the crowd with Warren, Ma, and Phoebe. Peter spotted us, and pointed our direction, while Terry waved the three of them over.

They tried to make their way over to us, but they kept getting stopped by people wanting to say hello to them, especially Ma and Phoebe. They had become mother figures to some of the guys during that time. That was how Warren's mom affectionately got the name Ma.

As they came over, some guys at a nearby table recognized them, and offered their chairs to Ma and Phoebe. Almost just as immediately Warren produced a joint and wanted me to go out to the alley for a toke.

Ma said, "I wish you wouldn't smoke that stuff."

"Aw Ma, it helps me eat because that stuff the doctor gives me makes me sick."

"I know," she said, "but I still don't like it."

Then she smiled at me. "Well, at least it's not alcohol. *That* stuff *is* poison."

So, out we went for a toke, afterward, I paid a quick visit to the washroom when we came back inside. When I got back to the table, there was a small crowd of guys gathered around Warren, Ma, and Phoebe. That always happened.

Lots of times Warren, Ma, Phoebe, Hunter, and I would arrive at the Royal, and while Hunter, Warren, and I'd be supping beer, Ma and Phoebe would have their coffee, tea, or soda. That's when we'd be joined by several of the guys from the BCPWA who would talk with Phoebe and Ma. All the guys got Mom-Hugs from both Ma and Phoebe.

Someone would be walking by and stop. "MA!" Then they'd give each other a hug.

Afterward, she'd smile shake her head. "I never thought I'd see the day when I would have a hundred sons."

"Yeah," said Phoebe, "or a hundred nephews!"

Phoebe's beading and leather work became especially popular. She was always sewing and beading a pair of moccasins or gloves, and that kept her busy. She made a tidy sum of money doing it. There were always guys wanting her to make them something traditional for themselves or gifts. Warren mentioned that in his book:

> One of the owners of the Royal heard about Phoebe's work and gave her a fucking nice commission to make a beautiful vest with fringes and beadwork. The owner was so blown away by it, he seriously considered putting it in a frame rather than wear it. No lie.

The Christmas of 1990 was special. As I recall, it was after the three of them had been volunteering at BCPWA for a while, and it was getting close to the Christmas Season. Phoebe suggested we host an Orphans Christmas for the guys who were going to be alone on that day. These were mostly gay and bi men who were not only rejected by their families for being Queer, but HIV/AIDS as well.

We had a few guys stay over Christmas Eve. Some went to midnight Mass, then came back here for Christmas treats and hot chocolate, while some had a shot of Christmas cheer before bed.

The main event happened the next day with our kitchen full of willing guests to help make breakfast and dinner. Warren supervised the whole thing. Then after breakfast was had, everyone got presents, some lunch was served, and then dinner preparations were underway.

I remember there was one guy who worked with Warren at the BCPWA, a sweet little guy named Shane, felt really close to Ma. His own parents were quite religious and had disowned him when they found out that he was gay and HIV positive as well. Ma and he would often talk together while she was at the office volunteering.

At one point that Christmas Eve, he and Ma were talking, and he was telling her about how lonely he felt this time of year, especially after being rejected by his family. He told her how he considered us his family.

He looked at Ma, kind of chuckled, and asked, "Will you be my mom?"

She hugged him and said, "I am your ma, whether you like it or not!" The two of them laughed till they cried and stayed in their embrace. Some of the guys gathered around for a group hug.

The other reason I remember that Christmas so well was dinner time. Everyone had been sitting at the table waiting for dinner, while four of the guys were in the kitchen putting the finishing touches on the turkey dinner. Two of them brought the bird from the kitchen on a big wooden tray decked out in holiday resplendence. That's when one of them, who was wearing socks, slid on the hardwood floor, and the whole presentation crashed. Some laughed, while others panicked a bit. I especially remember hearing Phoebe's infectious laugh above everybody else. One of the guys at the table had his camera handy and took pictures. So, we salvaged what we could and had a wonderful Christmas meal despite it all.

That incident was the talk of BCPWA for a good couple of months afterward. And the photos that were taken of the turkey fallout were posted on the office bulletin board. I now have possession of one of the copies of that photo, complete with the pinholes from when it was on the bulletin board, and I take it out every Christmas season.

Kelly and Gord showed up to help us out. In a very short time, we'd become friends. They helped us out with providing extra food and helping us to decorate the place.

I remember we had twenty-four guests for Christmas dinner, and enough leftovers to last for, what seemed like a month! And that was *after* everybody took leftovers home with them!

Isn't it funny how one can smile and cry at the same time? That's what these memories do to me.

14

The whole Gay Games week was filled with all kinds of activity. There were sporting events all over Vancouver and suburbs like Burnaby. I was too busy to attend any of them at the time, with rehearsals and playing gigs into the night. In fact, through my talk with Terry, my band, Hamstring managed to score four weeknights at the Royal that week. The crowds were better than usual because of the folks in town for the Games. I would have preferred that we had landed weekend gigs because they were bigger crowds and more money, but a couple of other bands got those time slots because it was on a first-come, first-serve basis. I was still grateful that we were able to get in during the week the Games were on.

We would introduce ourselves as *the only local gay band we know of*, and that seemed to get a lot of positive reaction from the crowds. We even invited Auntie Vivian to sing with us for a few of the numbers in her full tough drag. And Auntie Vivian had never met a microphone that she didn't like. Besides, she was a huge hit! Especially when she would sing her band's hit song "Up Your Ass" and an old punk/blues song from the 1970s by Trans-Punk performer Jayne County, called "(If You Don't Want to Fuck Me, Baby), FUCK OFF!!"

The crowds loved Auntie Vivian, and she had the patrons yelling FUCK OFF at the appropriate moments during the song. She was so popular that she ended up singing with us all week long. She was like Divine while she sang, with her teased wig, tight fitting dresses, outrageous makeup, and stiletto heels. Her interactions with the audience ranged from being a potty mouth to wandering into the audience grabbing guys by the ass and cupping their crotches. It was fantastic! The audience loved her, and we made a shitload of money in tips that week.

Vancouver's annual Gay Pride Parade took take place during the Games. Hunter had volunteered to be part of the security team and had to leave early that morning to be in the West End to get things ready. This, after getting home at around five thirty or six after being out all night.

He had a quick shower, swallowed a quick gulp of coffee, then bolted out the front door. Meanwhile, Ma and Phoebe showed up while Warren was in the shower.

After having some coffee and chocolate chip bannock Phoebe had baked, we all got ready and went downtown. We eventually found a place to sit on a small rise looking down onto Sunset Beach with a decent view of all the kiosks and the stage for the after-parade show. When we arrived, Warren had to leave to go down to the kiosk where the BCPWA was so he could start his volunteer shift.

There were literally *thousands* of people all around us. We saw so many people we hadn't seen in a long time, and of course, Ma and Phoebe were lovingly surrounded by some of the guys from BCPWA.

After being in the beating mid-summer sun for a while, we sought some cooling off. We walked up the hill from Sunset Beach to Davie Street and caught a bus back to the East End. And all too soon, the day was over, and we were back at home. Ah, peace and quiet at last.

15

"So, what part of the book are you going to be reading tonight?" Brady asks.

"You know, I've had a hard time trying to figure that one out," I say. "I'm in a bit of a panic inside because I can't seem to decide, and yet it will only be in a few hours that I'll be up in front of an audience reading something."

"You should make up your mind, Papi. Times ticking away."

"That's what I'm concerned about, there are a lot of passages in this book that I'm sure the audience would enjoy, I just can't seem to settle on one."

"Do you have a time limit on what you're reading?"

"Five minutes."

"Maybe pick a short one, and read it while I time it, and we can see how it fits."

"That's a good idea."

I quickly page through the book and come upon a passage.

"Okay, you ready?"

"Stand by," he says, then he signals me. "…and GO!" He starts the timer on his phone while I read.

> It was the last day of the Gay Games, and I was up making coffee for everyone real early. Eventually, everybody appeared in the kitchen. When we'd all had our coffees and showers, we went downtown to join some of our friends for breakfast. After that, we dropped Gil and Neil off in Yaletown. They were going to see a play called Quarantine of the Mind.

Daryl and me came back home with Auntie Vivian and Hunter where we smoked a joint. It must have been the pot because the conversation became real philosophical. I listened while everyone talked about the fact that people, regardless who they are or where they come from, were in the process of taking back their personal power… or some shit like that.

Auntie Vivian said that he had never given away his personal power in the first place. In fact, now, especially with his tough drag persona on stage, he feels more powerful than ever. She's got balls!

After our Kierkegaard-and-tokes-session (as Daryl called it), we piled in the car, picked up Ma and Phoebe over at their place, and went down to a craft fair at the Plaza of Nations before the Closing Ceremonies. There were lineups everywhere, so we decided just to go on ahead to BC Place Stadium.

Wow! What an experience the Closing Ceremonies were. Such a feeling of warmth everywhere. The entertainment for the evening included an address by the national Justice Minister Kim Campbell and entertainment by blues artist Long John Baldry and the Nylons. Once again, comedian Robin Tyler was the MC for the evening. What a show!

I heard tell that the teams from Berlin East Germany really enjoyed themselves a lot. After the fall of the Berlin Wall a year ago, they were getting their first taste of the total freedom to celebrate being Queer!

The Fourth International Gay Games are going to be in New York City in 1994. It was kind of emotional to know that this has really come to an end.

After the Closing Ceremonies, we went to the Plaza of Nations where an after-ceremonies party was being held. Folks were packed like sardines! People… everywhere! Line ups… everywhere, for food, for booze, and from what we were hearing, every single bar downtown had lineups out the doors and down the streets.

> Bert and Neil arranged to meet some of their friends from Toronto there, so they stayed. Me and Ma were feeling really tired, so Phoebe and Daryl took us home. I was ordering a pizza, when Hunter and Auntie Vivian came in, so I ordered a second one. We all sat up and bullshitted for a while, ate pizza, and we were all in bed by 1AM.
>
> Sleep didn't come easy that night because the people across the street were up partying and hooting and hollering at three thirty in the morning. Then, just as Bert and Neil were getting back from downtown, the folks across the street started a small fire outside of their house. It got going really good and caught onto one of the corners of the house, which began burning the exterior wall real quick. The cops and fire department were called, and they had it out in no time! And a Vancouver Police Department carted a few of the partygoers away.

"Three minutes." Brady smiles while stopping his phone. "I like that passage."

"I don't know, it's too short. I'll have to think about that."

"You could always shock all the family-types who will be there and read that scene where you and he have sex in the prison showers when nobody's around."

I laugh. "Do you think I would get me invited back after reading something like that?"

"Maybe not, but they'll probably be talking about it for quite a while afterwards."

"Well, yeah, that's for sure."

16

Then there was *this* that followed directly after the last passage. I don't read it out to Brady, but of course I don't have to read it to remember it.

It was the day after the Closing Ceremonies of the Gay Games, Sunday morning. We were up and at it by nine, coffee went on and Bert and Neil were just getting out of bed, when a phone call came through from Kelly and Gord.

They were hosting a spur-of-the-moment party at their place that afternoon, for an American crew that were filming the Gay Games. Well, that sounded like a lot of fun, so I told him we'd be there. I didn't have to convince anybody. We all showed up at three, and what a party it was! It wasn't only the American film crew who were there, but all these folks from all over the world, and their house was just packed! Most of the film crew were from Philadelphia, and there were members of the various teams from all over the world!

Kelly introduced Ma and Phoebe to two young Māori guys from New Zealand, and the four of them were like instant long-lost cousins. They spent the entire party in a corner talking, relating stories and experiences, and laughing together.

I got talking to quite a few people: there was this hilarious woman named Jocelyn, from Boston, and a couple from Scotland named Seamus and Kevin that I got talking to about politics. Then there was a couple from Amsterdam

> named Jan and Pieter. (Pieter was cute, horny little bastard—every time he'd pass me, he would grab my crotch and wink at me while going by. I didn't mind one bit.)
>
> Then there was this guy Felix, an actor from San Francisco, who turned out to be a real hoot. He was really animated and loud when he talked, and the more he drank the louder, and more hilarious he was. Auntie Vivian and him hit it right off and kept the party going all afternoon.
>
> Anyways, Kelly and me spent about an hour talking about the CDs in his collection. He was playing albums by groups I'd never heard of before and I really liked what I was hearing. Stranglers 10 was one of the more popular ones he was playing that afternoon. He played it a couple of times after folks asked for it.

I would have remembered that night even if Warren hadn't written about it, but because he did there is an extra richness to the memory. It was a terrific experience. Everybody left around six or six thirty—many had planes to catch.

The two young Māori guys gave Ma and Phoebe an invitation to New Zealand to meet with Māori elders in Rotorua on the North Island. All the way back home they talked about the two, young handsome Māori men and their invitation to New Zealand. It was good to see them so excited.

To this day, I can't listen to *Stranglers 10* without thinking about that party.

During the ten-day event, there were only two—count 'em, *two*—incidences of violence. Now, as unfortunate as they were, there are other places in North America, or the world for that matter, where the casualty list would have been higher, much higher.

As gay people, we took our power back beautifully during Gay Games III. It was exhilarating to know that the City of Vancouver supported us in our efforts. We officially reclaimed our dignity and we'll never let it go again! The excitement, the celebration, the camaraderie after almost a decade's worth of living under the mushroom cloud of AIDS.

That whole event was a respite to remember who we are as a community and celebrate it. It gave us the opportunity to reaffirm ourselves to ourselves and become a stronger community for it.

We realized that, yet again, we would show the world the strength in our resolve and our numbers, and the fact that we are still here, we're still queer, and we're not going anywhere *despite* AIDS, bitches!

Unfortunately, this was also the time when Warren's illness had advanced to such a point where he watched the entire ceremony while wearing his mooshum's jacket because he was always cold even though it was August. His face was getting a little gaunt, and looked a little wasted, but none of that dampened his spirit.

Ma wasn't doing well either. By this time, she was using a walker because she was finding it more difficult to get around. She was also becoming more dependent on us just for the day-to-day things. Besides her cancer, I guess the stress of being beaten by her ex-husband, losing Warren, and then the stress she felt searching for him for all those years had really taken a toll on her.

She liked Bert right away. Warren had told her how he and Bert looked out for each other the first time he went to jail. When she was introduced to him, she hugged and kissed him. Then she said, "So you're Bert. Warren has always spoken of you with such respect. Thank you for looking after my son while you two were inside."

For the entire time they were here, she treated Bert like her own son.

17

It wasn't too long after the Gay Games that Warren's health went haywire. As I recall, it began happening in late September of 1990. Warren became quite sick and sequestered himself to bed for a couple of days. He was having trouble breathing. We were all worried. Actually, we were frightened! It came on so fast that we weren't sure what to do. So, the three of us—Ma especially—stuck close by the house so we could care for him.

A couple of days passed, and Warren was in terrible shape. After every third word he spoke, he had to take a deep breath, and he looked emaciated. We took him to Dr. Chu who suspected that it was pneumocystis pneumonia (or PCP) a fungal lung infection that folks with compromised immune systems are susceptible to.

Warren was admitted to Saint Paul's Hospital immediately. He had a lot of trouble breathing. After Warren was settled into his room, Dr. Chu recommended nobody but Ma, Phoebe, Hunter, and I visit Warren until late in the week so he could rest. Warren was frightened and kept repeating how he didn't want to die. We gathered close around him.

Over that week, Warren gradually started looking a lot better than he had when we brought him in although he was still having difficulty breathing.

Then, one evening we arrived at Saint Paul's Hospital to see him, the door to his room was closed. We asked the nurse on duty what had happened, and apparently, he had a rough afternoon and really didn't want to see anybody, so we left the stuff we brought for him with the nurse. Next, we heard he then got a fever and was in rough shape again.

Over the next couple of days, we went to see him, and he was looking better than he'd looked all week. His temperature was stable, and he was able to leave the next day.

When he got back home, the next couple of days were a real challenge because he was really down and got into an uncharacteristically foul mood—plus, he was covered in a rash. We discovered later that both his mood and the rash were directly related to the medication he was taking. When his doses were adjusted, he started looking a lot better. Healthier (and happier). And so, began a quick recovery.

But it was ultimately a period of grace that wasn't going to last long. None of us had any illusions either, least of all Warren.

In less than six months, it would be all over.

During his last few weeks, we talked a lot about what I was going to do after the inevitable day of his passing. Of course, I told him I'd be sad and lonely. But then we talked about his journals, the book that he was writing, and the fact that he gave it over to me to finish for him. I accepted that responsibility, even though I had no idea what to do with it—or if I really wanted it in the first place. But I also knew that he was in no condition to finish it. I took that to heart and set about that task of finishing putting that book together and publishing it.

Warren succumbed to PCP in March 1991. I arrived home from rehearsal one evening and there was a message left on the answering machine from Hunter. Warren was taken back to Saint Paul's Hospital earlier that evening. I somehow knew this would be his final exit.

Hunter told me what ward Warren was on, so I phoned the ward and the nurse told me he was very weak and resting.

A lot of that weekend was spent visiting with Warren in the hospital. But I wasn't quite prepared to see the state he was in when I first entered the room. I never noticed how damn skeletal he'd become. It happened so quickly! He was, at times, heavily medicated, and his voice even sounded different. He had tubes running here and there, and he'd get confused and his voice would trail off a lot. He couldn't walk by himself, and he got tired easily.

The next afternoon, after seeing Warren in the hospital, Ma, Phoebe, Hunter, and I went for dinner. We all somehow knew this was it, Warren would not be coming home anymore.

When we got back to our place, there was a phone message from Dr. Chu wanting us to call him back. It was with great dread that I returned Dr. Chu's call. He told me that Warren had passed away at five thirty that afternoon. I felt numb. That's all I can remember feeling at the time. The four of us sat in silence for the longest time, letting it sink in. Ma started crying, and before we knew it, the four of us were hugging each other and crying.

18

Throughout those early years of loss and grieving, both in Vancouver and New Zealand, the promise I made to Warren was never far from my thoughts. I knew I was not going to escape *Last Chance Town*, and so piece by piece I set to work. It was a project of fits and starts, and there were days—even weeks and months—where frustration kept me from accomplishing much.

But chapter by chapter, memory by memory, things started to take shape.

And then it happened! And when things finally started to click, the pieces fell into place quickly. Like a band that enjoys "overnight success" after years of playing bar gigs—after several years of organizing and sending submissions out to publishers, the manuscript was finally picked up by Curious Badger Publishing, a small independent out of Ottawa. Once that happened, its forward momentum took it over the finish line, and *Last Chance Town* became an actual published book!

I remember cracking the tape on my box of copies, opening the flaps, lifting out some brown craft paper, and… well, there it was—the book that Warren wrote during the last two years of his life.

I picked it up and skimmed through it, feeling Warren's approval and gratitude.

It'd been a long row to hoe.

By the time the project was fully in gear home computers became ubiquitous, so I had bought a Mac and started by transcribing his journals. That in and of itself was a major feat. The chicken scratch that had been his writing was something to behold, and something more to interpret. Many times, I would have to re-read his sentences several times to decipher it, often more from context than anything else. Then came the task of editing as much as I could make sense of.

While I was doing that, I was asking some of my musician and artist friends about how to go about publishing a book. I got a lot of different answers as to the proper way of approaching publishing, and when I thought the moment was right, I sent the manuscript to potential publishers. It became a bizarre ritual. I'd send out the manuscript with a return envelope because I wanted the script back, and *months* later, I would get the manuscript back with a Thanks-but-No-Thanks letter.

"So, it goes," as Vonnegut used to say.

All the way along, I had people to help out with the publishing process. I remember Layton, one of the editors at Curious Badger Publishing, turned out to be really helpful. I remember when he first edited the manuscript and returned it to me, it was so full of red marks and editing symbols that I thought I was going to have to rewrite the entire thing! But he assured this was not the case. And he went over the first couple of pages of editing, and he was right—it wasn't as bad as it originally looked.

Once I got through the editing, the front cover had to be designed. The marketing department came up with three possible designs for the book, and it was hard for me to choose which ones I liked. But I eventually went with the design that presently adorns the front cover. Then they wanted me to come up with a summary of what the book was about, and a small biography for Warren.

That was the toughest part. How to make people want to read the book, without giving too much away? How do I put a general plot of a book in a small paragraph or two (or three) and still leave some mystery to it? After numerous tries, this is what I came up with for the back cover:

> Life on the street is crazy, even more crazy when you're young and should be in school. But there's nothing at the

foster home for you to go to, and the folks on the street feel more like family anyway. Most of all, the people who are supposedly looking out for you—social services—think you're just a stupid *Métis* kid! Then you end up in jail... twice! Then you discover that you're HIV Positive. What now?

This is Warren Givens' story. The man I met one night at a gay bar in Vancouver, BC, the man who came home with me, and stayed. The man who I fell in love with and through whom I gained a whole new family with his ma and her cousin Phoebe.

It's also a trip to a place and time, the late 1980s and the year 1990, scarily turbulent and yet exhilarating times in the Gay Community. A personal account of what happened and how everything in our community was affected.

Jeez, not bad, I remember thinking as I read over the final draft. *That kind of says it all.*

19

It'll be my turn soon, and the palms of my hands are clammy, which I don't understand because I'm a musician, and I've performed in front of audiences for years! I should be used to this! But I'm thinking that maybe I'm feeling this way because I'm presenting a portion of Warren's book for the first time tonight, so it's quite personal.

The passage that I've finally chosen to read, clocks in at about five and a half minutes, so I hope the MC lets me finish it and not stop me when I'm almost through.

My eyes dart back and forth over the audience, must be fifty or sixty of them sitting out there listening to us. I can see Brady sitting in the front row. He looks at me, smiles and gives me a thumbs-up. I smile and blow him a kiss.

We're sitting at a long table at the front of a packed room facing the audience, while a young woman with fluffy pink hair is at the mic. She's finishing reading a poem about wild, windy Wednesdays and bad hair. The audience is splitting a gut laughing. She says a few more lines as she finishes reading, thanks the audience and sits down to applause.

Bill, the MC for the night, steps up to the mic. "Thanks Sylvia, and that was terrific. And now, reading from *Last Chance Town*, a memoir by Warren Givens, is the man who helped produce the book. Please welcome Daryl Kellerman."

In my nervousness, I can barely hear the audience clap as I get up to adjust the mic a bit higher… and drop the book from my hand.

"SHIT!" I accidently say into the mic. Several in the audience members laugh. I smile and wave knocking the mic stand over. More people laugh.

Bill comes over and helps me get myself straightened up. I make a last-minute adjustment, find the bookmarked page, and address the audience.

"As Bill told you, I'm not Warren Givens, he passed away this very day back in 1991. People have been asking me about this jacket I'm wearing tonight, it belonged to Warren, his grandmother originally made it for his grandfather.

"It was especially important to Warren that this book be published. He wanted people to know about him—his life and his dreams—because he felt he never had a chance to live the life he really wanted. He wanted his book to be a testament to others to pursue their dreams and have the courage to live the life of their dreams.

"Before he died, he passed this project on to me to finish, and I am really pleased and honoured to be reading a portion of it to you this evening."

The audience applauds.

> It's Saturday, August 4, 1990, and the third annual Gay Games opens tonight here in Vancouver! There are over seven thousand athletes, from twenty-eight different countries, plus an expected extra sixteen thousand spectators coming!
>
> Daryl and me got up, and I had a shower. Then we went to meet Phoebe and Ma for breakfast at a restaurant called Jukebox Johnny's Diner on West Broadway.
>
> On our way there, we stopped in at the Orpheum Theatre downtown, and I bought five tickets to the opening ceremonies at BC Place tonight. They were $23.50 per ticket.
>
> Afterward, while we were coming through the front door at home, the phone was ringing, and it was Bert and Neil from Toronto! They'd arrived in town and were having some fish and chips somewhere on Davie Street. They were telling

me how much being in the West End brought back memories of that trip we took together in 1983! They said they were coming over to our place afterward because they're staying with us for the next couple of weeks.

Me, Daryl, and Hunter hurried around and did some last-minute clean-up type things, then they showed up. After I introduced everybody, we had a sit-around-and-bullshit session with beer and tokes, then we went back downtown.

Daryl parked his car by the corner of Davie and Jervis in the Gay Village, and Neil went to Little Sister's Bookstore to have a look around. Bert told me that he heard about a place called Mack's Leathers on Granville Street and wanted to see it. I couldn't help it, I told him I knew where it was.

"So, Bert, you guys are into some kinky shit, are ya?"

He smiled at me and didn't say nothing.

When we finally arrived there, I was watching a cute guy looking at some tit rings, when his friend came over with a paddle and gave his ass a love tap. A tough looking woman who was behind the counter drinking beer from a can.

"Here," she said, "I'll show you how it works."

Then she grabbed the paddle from the guy, ordered a young woman wearing a collar who was standing nearby, to bend over the counter. The young woman smiled, went over to the counter, pulled up her denim skirt to show her bare ass. That's when the tough woman gave her a couple of loud WHACKS with the paddle. The woman with the collar stood up, pulled her skirt down and quietly walked back to where she had been standing. Then the woman with the paddle, turned to the two guys.

"Nice shade of red, eh?"

The two guys couldn't get out of the store fast enough. I laughed.

Bert bought a couple of wrist restraints and then we went back to the car to meet Neil. I kidded him about being a kinky old shit now.

"You must have learned that when we were inside," I said.

He just smiled again. And didn't say nothing.

We came back home, so they could get a couple of hours' sleep.

That's when Auntie Vivian showed up from Portland because he was staying with us for the duration of the Games too. Daryl, me, Hunter, and Auntie Vivian shot the shit for and little bit then I had a quick shower. And Bert and Neil got out of bed and got ready too.

We were finally off to the Opening Ceremonies of the Gay Games. Daryl parked his car beside BC Place Stadium, and we went out to mingle.

What a Thrill! A stadium full of gay folks from all over the world! Together in one place, celebrating our love! ALL FUCKING RIGHT!!

The MC was Robin Tyler, and she was excellent! The first openly gay Member of the Canadian Parliament, Svend Robinson, stole the show, and there were musical appearances by Carole Pope from the band Rough Trade and Lorraine Segato from the band Parachute Club.

We saw all kinds of people that we all knew, and Bert and Neil bumped into some of their friends from Toronto. This whole show just blew me away. But it went on a bit too long, (four and a half fucking hours).

Daryl, Bert, Neil, Auntie Vivian, Hunter, and me went to Streets, a pub at the Dufferin Hotel, and we all had a beer while Bert had a coffee.

"You still a caffeine addict, Bert?" I asked.

"Yeah, you know me."

Daryl had a bit too much to drink, so Bert drove us all to our place.

Before I know it, I'm thanking an appreciative audience whose applause accompanies me to my seat. It's done. Weeks of anticipation and nerves simply fall away.

As the evening winds down, once all the readers had presented, I'm talking with members of the audience and being congratulated. I am engaging with strangers, accepting all kinds of compliments, and fielding questions as to the type of guy Warren was. I sign several copies of the book purchased by audience members getting a little tipsy on the wine and cheese that the publishers provided everybody. Wow! What a night!

Brady finally catches up with me, kisses me, and tells me that I read well. I thank him and we agree that maybe it's time to go home. He gets on his cell phone and orders a cab, they tell him it will be about thirty minutes, so a little more time to do some schmoozing and glad-handing about the book.

20

The taxi pulls up in front of the apartment building. As Brady pays the driver, I get out, and a car drives by with "New Orleans is Sinking" by the Tragically Hip flooding from the wide opened window. I stop and think about Warren again and how he loved the Tragically Hip. I can still hear his voice when he first heard them.

"Holy shit man, these guys are fuckin' fantastic! I'm gettin' this album!" And he did, and I've loved this song ever since!

We enter the lobby to see Conrad vacuuming the rug… late at night as usual. He sports his usual sullen look on his face, and I swear he has one shirt to his name. A white T-shirt with the words GET A GRIP! emblazoned down the front in bold lettering.

"Feelin' better tonight, Conrad?" I ask.

He just shakes his head. "Sometimes I feel like I'm nothin' but a bloody serf around here!"

That's Conrad. I feel a smirk on my face as we go over and summon the elevator. As we ride the lift to the fourteenth floor, Brady and I kiss, and I realize just how tired I feel right now.

"It looks like tonight is going to be an early night," I say.

"That's alright by me."

Inside the apartment, we shed jackets and boots, and I pour us a special drink. Then I slide an old CD in the player I still have after all these years. It just so happens that "New Orleans is Sinking" by the Tragically Hip cascades out of my speakers in honour of Warren.

I hand Brady his drink, and pick up Warren's book from the coffee table, and turn over to the end to the last entry he ever made.

"I want to read you one more thing from this book," I say. "It's really short."

"Okay."

I turn the music down. "When Warren wrote this, he could barely write because he was really weak, so it was hard for me to read when I transcribed it from his journal:

> It's four thirty-five in the afternoon. I've been having a real hard time breathing lately. I have to sit almost straight up most of the time so I can have a chance to breathe proper-like, all the time! I got this oxygen mask attached to me a lot of the time, and it's fucking annoying! I'm tired, and all I want to do is sleep.

"He died about an hour after he wrote this."

We're both silent.

I go over and look out the living room window to the cold March evening. Brady joins me, and I put my arm around his shoulders. I raise my glass. "To Warren," I say. "He never got to know just how much of a special person he really was. I love him and always will."

"To Warren," Brady says.

We both raise our glasses and take a sip, then look over to the apartment buildings that overlook English Bay, and they seem to be settling down for the night as the individual lights of each apartment illuminates the cool night.

"Well," I say, "at least it's not raining."

Thank You

James Howard: for appearing in my life just when meeting somebody special was the furthest thing from my mind. I'm so glad you're a big part of my life, and I love you.

My editor Warren Layberry (also, hi Renée). Thanks for all the amazing suggestions and the pep talks over coffee all this time. I could not have completed this novel without your help and guidance.

Cassie Smith, Elliott Hockley, Maria Brown, Chelsea Rutherford, and all the folks at Tellwell Press for your invaluable assistance with marketing myself with this book.

Zoe Duff and all the folks at Filidh Publishing in Victoria, BC, for all your encouragement and support!

The members of Canadian Authors–BC, again, for the encouragement and support.

The good folks at the Vancouver Métis Community Association, especially J. Paul Stevenson, Ken Pruden, Marshal Loewen, Don MacDonald, June Scudeler, Laura Baird from Tsawwassen First Nation, the John Howard Society Lower Mainland, and all the community volunteers who shared my journey in working with the offenders.

To Jessie and David Blair, Lloyd Nicholson, Kelly Mahoney, Turner Smith, Michael Woodman, Jim Ahlers, Rosa Venditti, Gary Smiley, Brad Andrews, Kempton Dexter, Len Aruliah, Wendy Schultenkamper and Chantal-Annick Desrosier, Wendy Johnson and Lynn Tuthill, and all the many folks who believed in me and supported me through all these years.

To my many cohorts of Peter Sage's EMF Cohort 12! You folks are the best! I am truly blessed and grateful. Thank you.

CPSIA information can be obtained
at www.ICGtesting.com
Printed in the USA
BVHW041255080922
646521BV00002B/136